# A Little
# Breathing Room

# A Little
# Breathing Room
## *by* Richard Graber

Harper & Row, Publishers
New York, Hagerstown, San Francisco, London

Library of Congress Cataloging in Publication Data
Graber, Richard.
    A little breathing room.

    SUMMARY: A teenage boy growing up in Minnesota in
1935 is frustrated in his attempts to contend with
his manipulative family.
    [1. Family life—Fiction.    2. Fathers and sons—
Fiction]    I. Title.
PZ7.G749Li    [Fic]    77-25658
ISBN 0-06-022059-7
ISBN 0-06-022060-0 lib. bdg.

For Pop and the living memory
of Mom
with special love to
Rebecca, Nancy, and John

# 1

"Bud, sometimes I'd really like to clobber you, you know that? I mean really *clobber* you. Now come on!"

"Go ahead, sock me. You're the big brother."

"I can't do that and you know it. Honest to Pete, now you've got your hair slicked down with water and it'll freeze by the time we get to Karsten's. He'll like that for sure, icy hair dripping all over the studio. If you don't want to do it, *say* so."

"I don't want to *do* it! I *said* I—"

"Yah, well, it's too late now. Come on, before Mom gets home. Jeez!"

My kid brother, for an eight-year-old, is the stubbornest . . . well, for any-year-old, as far as that goes. He looks small for his age but he isn't. He's just sort of squat and solid. Not fat; low and wide. Hard to move.

Like this thing. I thought it was a good idea. I *still* think it's a good idea. Take some of the money I got for helping on Hansords' farm during threshing and get Bud to put in some of his allowance. He *saves* his allowance, can you beat that? Anyway, get our picture taken. I mean by Mr. Karsten down at the studio by Fenster's barbershop, not a snapshot. I checked. We can afford three five-by-sevens and give two to Mom and Dad for Christmas and one to Grandpa and Grandma.

But we've got to hurry now and get Bud changed and get down to Karsten's before Mom gets back from bridge club, and Bud won't wear his shirt and tie.

"Come on, it's just for half an hour or so and you'll have your winter coat on. Nobody'll see. For gosh sakes, just put on your white shirt and that elastic tie!"

"No."

My brother looks like a bullterrier right now, nothing against bullterriers.

"Bud, why *not,* for crying out loud? I'm wearing *mine.*"

"My Sunday shirt and the tie Mom gave me?"

"Yah, exactly. Okey-dokey?"

Hey, maybe he'll come around. Maybe he'll—

"Nope. I'll wear the flannel shirt."

"Jeez, Bud, why not. Just tell me why not!"

" 'Cause I'll die. I'll be killed and then you'll be sorry and—"

"I won't be. . . . *Nobody* gets killed from wearing a white shirt, ya jerk."

"Oh yes they do, yes they do, if somebody grabs it from behind and pulls it tight and your eyes pop out and roll in the snow and you try to get loose but you can't see, and you try to stay alive and make it back to the cabin where you've got the killer hatchet and the poison but you can't make it because of the blood and—"

"Oh for Pete's sake, get up off the floor and put the flannel shirt on then! I don't care."

He stands up and stretches his arms out and pokes his belly out as far as he can, which is pretty far, and he grins like a ninny.

"It *is* on, Ray. I'm wearing it. See?"

"Yah, well *keep* it on then!"

So after all that, he comes out of the bathroom with the wet hair and there he stands, dripping. Nobody in the whole town of Rock River goes outside with wet hair, not in the winter. Good Lord, this is Minnesota and it's December 10, 1935, and this December it's *cold*.

Anyway, we get it done, don't ask me how. We wound up with four to pick from, and only one would work because Bud screwed up his face one time and looked cross-eyed another time. He's very good at that. And one time he looked just plain mean. But the last one wasn't bad; he just looked sort of not interested. Probably tired out. So we picked that one, or *I* did. He wanted the cross-eyed one. A comedian. And he didn't even catch cold. He never does.

So at Christmas, Grandma and Grandpa came out from Minneapolis on the train and they were really pleased, I could tell. They said the picture was good of Jefferson, too. *Jefferson.* That's Bud's real name, but don't ever call him that unless you're his grandma or something. Dad and Mom liked the pictures, too, I guess, and Dad started out on this responsibility thing he keeps after me about.

He looks at the picture again without cracking a smile. Then he leans back in the armchair and says, "Raymond, this shows *initiative,* yessir. Shows *enterprise.*"

"It does?"

"Darn betcha it does. Shows responsibility, and you'll need plenty of that if you're going to get ahead in the world, take my word for it."

"Yah, well, okay. Thanks."

So I let myself feel pretty good about the silly pictures. Everybody's sort of smiling, even Dad. I should know better. He looks up with that get-down-to-business look, takes off his spectacles, and says, "But Raymond, Bud should really be wearing a white shirt and tie, same as you. I'm surprised you didn't see to it."

"Well, we talked about—"

"No no." He raises his hand up like a kid in school who has to go to the bathroom. "No excuses now. You had plenty of time, you won't deny that!"

"No, but—"

"Well then. And you *knew* Bud should dress up."

"Yes, but—"

Then Mom says, "Oh Frank, I'm sure Ray tried."

"Well trying isn't enough, Laura. If a thing's

worth doing, it's worth doing *right.*"

Then he shut up. He wouldn't blow his stack with Grandma and Grandpa there. That's *his* folks. Mom's died before I was born even, and they lived I think in Chicago.

The thing is, Dad's *serious* about all this responsibility stuff and the business world. His dime store is the business world, I guess. Some world. You'd think I *purposely* had Bud wear a flannel shirt. All this time Bud sits cross-legged on the floor between the Christmas tree and the radio—a Philco console. He watches me but keeps his head down and looks up with his eyes, like a little old man. He grins, too, the rat.

*Dad* can't get Bud into a white shirt *ever,* because Bud starts screaming like a banshee and rolling on the floor and thrashing around until Dad says, "All right, *don't* wear the white shirt!" And Bud sits up with a grin and says, "Okay, Dad." That's mostly on Sunday mornings.

All at once I get this idea. I say it sort of easy.

"Dad, the thing is, we figured this would be better . . ."

"Better!"

"Yah, better, because you're all more used to seeing Bud in his flannel shirt, see. More lifelike, you might say."

"I see. Hmm. Yes."

And that satisfies him. Jeez! He nods his head and *looks* satisfied. What he doesn't think about is that they're all more used to seeing *me* in a flannel shirt, too, but I'm not about to bring it up. Bud and I each have another package to open, from Mom and Dad, only it looks like socks. "Nice warm socks" is what they'll say, but at least it'll keep Dad off the responsibility thing. And we can always use the socks, no question.

# 2

It's February, the coldest month of the whole year, in Minnesota anyway. Seems like every grownup in town talks about it, but it's never as cold as the winter of '26, or you name it. Well, this is February of 1936 and last week it hit thirty-two degrees below and the boiler at the school went kaflooey and we didn't have school for two days. Twice they couldn't get the buses out to pick up the farm kids for school, too.

But this morning looks good. It's seventeen below, but it's Saturday. Saturdays Bud and I sleep late, or pretend to, until Dad leaves for the dime store. He just left. He's lucky to still have the store, what with the Depression and all. It doesn't bring in much money, Mom says, but then nothing does these days. And she should know. She owns half the store and he owns the other half and she keeps the books. She keeps track of the money.

Still, lots of people would change places with Dad, no question. Like the men looking to work at a dollar and a half or even a dollar a day and not finding any. Not even on the farms, because the crops are pretty well shot. Lots of people are on relief, too, but they don't talk about it; they don't like handouts. Some fellows and even some whole families have left for California, especially farm families. Just take what they can, sell the rest for peanuts, and leave. Winter's no time to stick around here if you're so broke you can't buy coal or warm clothes.

Sometimes a farm lady will come into the store on Saturday night and trade a dozen of eggs or a chicken for thread and buttons and such. Mom told Dad to take it, which is probably a good idea. There's not much cash around, everybody knows that. And most everybody's in the same boat. Anyway, the grownups keep complaining and most of them complain about President Roosevelt, because this is Republican country out here, Dad said. Still, some of them jump at a chance to work on the WPA or go to a CCC camp. And electricity's coming through for the farms and that's the REA, Dad said. And all those things were thought up by the President. Well, folks have got to complain about something besides the weather.

Wow, it's cold in the attic. The window in our attic room is really frosted over. We get out of bed and I scrape a peephole and Bud scratches a whole route with his thumbnail and runs his finger over it.

"Admiral Byrd's lost," he says. He's wide awake and shivering. "He sees this deserted village right here and he thinks it's Little America but—"

"At the South Pole? He's lost?" Jeez, it's cold. Bud's on this Byrd thing. Admiral Richard E. Byrd, you bet. I mean Byrd flew over the Pole in 1929 from his camp that he called Little America. And then in '34 he stayed there alone for four or five months. Really. We used to try and listen to his reports by short-wave radio but you couldn't hear hardly anything except static and squeaks.

"Yup, he's lost all right, forty-eleven miles from the Pole and the village is the wrong one and he stops his dog sled and the lead dog starts barking like he knows there's one crazy explorer still left in the village and the guy sure enough comes out with a frozen beard down to his knees and he can't see because he's been inside the hut for fourteen years, but old Byrd doesn't know this, so—"

"Bud."

"Well, he doesn't. So the lead dog runs up and . . . the lead dog gets loose some way and runs up and licks the old guy's hand like crazy and they smile at each other and it turns out that—"

"Bud . . . *Bud.*"

"What."

"Come on. Jeez, it's cold up here. Let's get some breakfast."

We grab our pants and long johns and pull our patchwork quilts off the bed, wrap them around us, and go downstairs. Bud marches into the kitchen with his feet pointed straight ahead and his head down, and the quilt over his shoulders drags on the floor. He sits down like a tent and leans against the icebox.

The kitchen's warm and steamy. Smells like cinnamon and sugar. Mom's got her old apron on and she's got flour on her hands. Hey, it's potluck tonight. I clean forgot. Potluck supper at the church. That means going to the movies is out but I don't have the dime anyway, let alone an extra nickel for licorice sticks. Potlucks aren't the best things in the world but they're free because everybody brings something.

I pull my corduroys over my long underwear and put on the sweat shirt and the flannel shirt and the warm socks and Bud just sits there.

"Chief Long Winter need food," he says into the quilt. "Buffalo meat. Plenty buffalo meat. Squaw give Chief . . ."

"I'll give you a paddling, young man, if you don't pull on your underwear and get dressed," Mom says. "You'll catch your death. And one of you get the milk. Mr. Osborn came late this morning."

Bud starts with his long johns.

"Long Winter puts on white wolfskin. Only Chief puts on white wolfskin and what's going on here! Hey! I'm trapped. Mom, I'm sinking into the quicksand and . . . what's the matter with this goddamn thing anyway!"

He's snarled up in his long johns, clawing away like a cat in a gunnysack. Mom jerks the underwear up over his head. Hard.

10

"*Bud!* You've got your head where your behind's supposed to be, and no more of that talk around here. Now do it right, I'm busy."

It's true, he almost had his head through his drop seat. He lays the long johns out flat on the floor so he can climb in right.

Well, "one of you get the milk" means me, and when I open the front door and the storm door I have to squint. Not much snow, but the sun's already bright and the air's still and cold; I can feel it way down in my chest. The milk bottle's cold, too, but not frozen. Darn. Sometimes they freeze and push the milk cap up like a toadstool.

Our house is on a corner with a new curb in front and no curb on the side. A WPA curb is what it is. I can look up one street and down another. No street signs like they have in Minneapolis; we know where everybody lives. Mrs. Fenster, on the west corner, comes out on her back stoop and shakes a dry mop like she was killing a snake, but she pulls back inside in a hurry. She wears a sweater even in the summer. The streetlight isn't moving; it really is still. Usually the poor old streetlight hangs in the middle of the intersection and blows all over with the wind. We can tell it's a real blizzard when you can't see the streetlight from our living-room window. Not this morning, I mean at night.

I can hear some traffic out on the highway. Up towards Hedstroms' somebody's arguing about the weather. Barsteads' dog is barking down past Westlunds', as usual—a rat terrier I might just graze with a brick one of these days. Somebody on the other side of Fenster's is trying to start a Model A. Sounds like he won't make it, either. You can crank and crank but in this weather you've got to catch it the first time it sputters.

There's the tracks where Axel Torgerson got stuck last week. We had a thaw for a couple of days and it was easy to keep in the tracks in the slush— one set of tracks right down the middle of the street. But before they could get the scraper out and clear off the streets, it froze solid and snowed a little. Axel was driving his '34 Pontiac and he jumped the ruts to let Doc Wheeler go by in his new Buick, and he didn't get back in the tracks for an hour, swearing a blue streak all the time. I can even see where he threw down his big grain shovel. He came back on foot for that and slipped and cracked his elbow a good one. To top it off, his radiator boiled over. You could smell the alcohol for blocks.

There's Mr. Osborn coming over from Fenster's, picking his way. That's hard snow and ice, and slippery. Not much snow covering, just enough to make it tricky walking and keep the old folks inside, except the stubborn ones. The bottles jingle in his wire carrying basket. His horse breathes out steam, it looks like, and has little icicles all over his shaggy coat. Just shaggy in the winter. But then Mr. Osborn only uses him when the weather's bad. Good days he uses his Ford truck; it's faster and he can make the whole town in one trip, even up to the school.

"Morning, Ray. Cold enough for ya?"

"Sure is, Mr. Osborn."

"Yah well it's fresh, all right. Not like the winter of '22 by a long shot, but cold enough, you betcha. Say hello to your mother."

Mom's calling me to close the door and not heat all outdoors. Breakfast without Dad is nice on a Saturday, because there's not much arguing usually and we don't have to rush off to school. Half an orange and a bowl of oatmeal with the top milk on it and some brown sugar, one teaspoon. And cocoa. Not oranges *every* Saturday, just when they get some in. Mom pours off the top part of the milk for cream. It's not *really* cream, but pretty close. Also, it's scientific.

What I mean is every teacher I've ever had asks the class, "Which is heavier, cream or milk?" And you say cream even if you've been through it all before, and they say, "Aha, but if that's true then how does the cream rise to the top?" And everybody looks surprised and the teacher's happy for the whole day. I don't know what difference it makes, but I swear if I don't learn another thing in school I'm sure going to know that cream rises to the top. Which I knew anyway.

"Did you know that, Bud?" I ask him. "About cream rising?" He's pouring top milk into a hole in the middle of his oatmeal. "Did you?"

"No. Why?"

He looks at me like I'm queer in the head and I can't say that I blame him. Mom sits down and has a cup of coffee with us. She's got to get the angel food cake ready for the potluck. She always takes an angel food and we always have sponge cake the next day because you dasn't waste the egg yolks.

"Dad going with us tonight?"

"As far as I know, Ray. He'll probably close early. Not many customers in this kind of weather. You two be sure to bundle up now, and don't stay out too long."

"Why?" Bud asks.

*"Why?* Because it's cold out. Now don't be silly, Bud."

"No, why is Dad coming?"

Mom watches him shovel in the oatmeal.

"Because we're all going. *You've* been to potluck suppers. Families go as families and the Deckers are going to do just that. It's the least your father can do. I've got to get a move on."

"I ain't going."

Mom's lighting the gas range with a kitchen match and it puffs.

"What's that, Bud?"

"Come on, Bud, I'll sled you over to Benson's," I say. Benson's my best buddy. "Let's go."

A couple of minutes and we're outside. He looks like a pile of clothes on the sled, scarf wound around up to his eyes. Funny, but he *still* looks

14

sort of like an Indian chief. I drag him on the fool sled over to Benson's. The sounds are extra loud, the air's so cold and still. The runners screech on some icy gravel and make little sparks fly up. Not nearly enough snow for really good sledding.

Everything looks sort of wide open on a winter morning with the trees bare. From our place you can look up the street and past the frame and stucco houses, past the elms and cottonwoods and firs, and way across the valley to the west bluffs. Takes a good hour to hike out there, the valley's so wide. The snow—what there is of it—is dirty. Looks almost the color of the smoke coming out of chimneys. On this side of town quite a few of the houses still have barns out back from when they had horses, and they're fun to fool around in in the winter. Or summer. But they *look* cold.

And practically every *old* house has straw pitched up around the foundation and held down by laths for warmth. Right now, you can walk for blocks without finding a sidewalk shoveled off clean down to the sidewalk. People start walking in little paths and just keep doing it when it's this cold. It's easier, but it does get tricky. Feels more like snow now, it really does. The sky is getting gray even with the sun out.

Benson's not home, wouldn't you know. His mother tells us to come in and warm up but I tell her we just got out and she says he's probably up at Hammer's. Hammer's another buddy, sort of, but that's a pull up Semple Hill so I roll Bud off the sled. He rolls well.

"You said you'd pull me."

"Just to Benson's. Come on if you're coming; you can walk. Ya coming or not? And you're going to that potluck, you know."

He lags behind but he follows.

"And don't make a fuss to Dad about potluck."

"What if I do!"

"I'll clobber you, Bud, that's what."

"Oh no you won't."

He's right. I probably wouldn't. But he's thinking now and he knows he better shut up at dinner this noon. Shutting up he can do very well when he puts his mind to it.

Darn it, this is one of those days when nobody knows where anybody is. Hammer's not home, they don't know where. Nelson and Kernes hiked out to the quarry, they think. Shadow's supposed to be helping his old man at the icehouse, but I'll bet he isn't.

Coldest job in the world, getting those blocks of river ice into the iron harness. Then the putt-putt engine takes them up the tall chute dripping wet, and you push them off at the top and stack them inside in a lot of sawdust. It's like an old barn full of ice and sawdust, is what it's like, and those blocks stay frozen all through the summer. Oh heck, I *know* he isn't helping; not Shadow.

Some days you run into guys all over the place,

but this sure isn't one of them. Warming up some. Smells more like snow.

"Ray, we going home now?"

"Yah, come on. That's where we're going, or *I'm* going anyway. Should be almost dinner. You cold?"

"Naw."

He's frozen stiff but he won't say so. His scarf's all icy, but at least he's still got his mittens on. I hand him the sled rope.

"Here, Bud, grab ahold. I dragged the fool thing all over town practically, so you can drag it the last block."

Also, my fingers are numb where I grabbed the rope and I've got to wiggle them.

"There ain't enough snow."

"You figured that out, huh. Well, what in hell do you think I've been—"

"Hey Ray, look!"

He stops and points down the block at Gladys Westlund, a girl in my class who's not bad, really. I mean actually she's very nice and we're going steady, you might say. Like since Christmas vacation we've been to two Saturday matinees because her father wouldn't let us go to the movies at night. Neither would mine; I didn't even ask. And skating once and studying at her house once. All in a little over a month. I mean it's sort of understood that we're going steady. We haven't said so in so many words because, well, we just never seem to get around to that when we're together.

17

"Sure, Bud, it's Gladys. Who'd you think it was, Janet Gaynor or something?"

"She's looking this way!"

Bud's not exactly crazy about girls. Any girls. As a matter of fact, he got in plenty of hot water during the Christmas play rehearsals because he kicked three of them in the shin when they said he was cute, and one was the Virgin Mary. He was a shepherd who didn't say anything. Grandma said he did fine.

"Naw, she's just on her front steps. Probably checking the thermometer."

"Hi, Ray! Bud!" She waves and shouts, but not like a mad fool the way some of them do. "It's up to zero!"

Bud starts pulling the sled with his head down and he whispers, "Don't answer, Ray, don't say a word."

"Bud, don't be a sap. *Hi, Glad.*"

I can see now. Mr. Westlund is out in front, pouring a kettle of hot water in the radiator. A brand-new '35 Buick sedan with a radio, honest, and he lets the radiator freeze up on him. We don't have a car, but if we did . . . He runs back up and gives Gladys the kettle for more hot water. *That's* what she's doing.

Jeez, she's in a kimono or something. I've never seen her in . . . well, I've never seen *any* girl in her kimono like that. Just in the movies. It's pink. Jeez. And she waves.

Mr. Westlund says something to her and then swears at the car and she runs into the house. He isn't really crazy about me for some reason, so I just kind of half wave at him in case he's looking and expects it. It could be when I dropped the dictionary, I don't know.

I mean the time Gladys and I studied together in her living room and I dropped the dictionary. The big one off the stand. The stand fell over, too. We were looking up "wrath," which is towards the end, and everything crashed like a ton of bricks. Nothing broken though.

Old man Westlund stumbled into the living room without a shirt on, drying his face with a towel and yelling, "What the hell's going on here! What're you two up to anyway?"

We were both on the floor picking up the dictionary and stand. He looked around fast, like he expected the whole living room to be smashed to kindling. So I said, "Hi, Mr. Westlund. We were studying when—"

"Oh *Daddy!*" Gladys said. She sort of sobbed and ran past him—into the bathroom, I guess.

"Don't you 'Hi' me, mister, not after coming in and making a wreck of—"

"But we just had to look up 'wrath' and the dictionary slipped and—"

"I'll wrath *you,* Decker, if you don't haul ass out of here and I mean *now.* You want your dad to hear about this, is that what you want?"

"No, sir. I got to be going now."

I grabbed my jacket and books and hightailed it out the front door. He was in no mood for explanations. So Gladys and I didn't learn the definition. So what. The next day the word wasn't on the test anyway.

But that's why I sort of half wave to Mr. Westlund. Bud pulls my sleeve and says, "Dad's coming, Ray."

Bud sees him rounding the corner down past Westlunds' and we tear in our front door. No need to run, but it always makes things easier—well, most of the time—if we're home and ready for dinner when he gets there.

One thing about tramping all over town, you sure can work up a hunger. We put our mitts and stuff on newspapers to dry by the heat register; you can smell the hot wet wool. And we all sit down right at noon and Dad tears into dinner like there's no tomorrow, without a word. We all do. Salmon loaf and boiled potatoes, but anything tastes okay when you're hungry. Bud shovels away like he did with the oatmeal.

"What about tonight, Frank?" Mom asks. "Will you close early?"

"Hmm." He puts his spectacles down and wipes his mouth with the napkin still in the ring.

"Excuse me?"

"Yah. Yah, it looks like snow anyway. I'll be

here by six-thirty and you boys be ready—understand, Ray?"

"Sure." I give Bud the old evil eye and he keeps quiet.

The only other thing my father says before he goes back to the store is "Not decent, I tell you. Not decent at all. Ray, a person should know better; you should know better."

"About what?"

"You know what I mean, you know what I mean."

Actually, I don't have the faintest idea what he's—

"What I mean is, Christ Almighty, young girls these days, I just don't know. You'd think their parents would have enough sense to . . ."

And he's bundled up and out the door. Mom looks at me, shrugs her shoulders, and clears the table. He saw old Gladys in her pink kimono. Must have. My father's a crackerjack at leaving you hanging like that. I mean sometimes he just says half of what he'd like to, and other times he lets loose with something just as he's leaving the house or going into the bathroom.

Well, so what. Bud has to sweep the basement and I have to clean up our room and bring down the dirty clothes for Monday wash. Chores, you know, and they've got to be done right; Mom sees to that. At least she says what she's thinking.

It's getting darker and I can hear Bud through the register. He's down in the basement with the push broom. "Aha!" he says. "Gotcha cornered, so take *that* and *that!*" I'd rather not know what's going on. He checks mousetraps in the fruit cellar every morning and on Saturdays he puts out fresh scraps and sets the traps. He's pretty good at it. Thinks he's Frank Buck.

The wind's coming up, right off the Dakotas, starting to spit snow. Bud and I horse around with some card games later, and he beats me at Authors because I'm sick and tired of Alfred Lord Tennyson and Edgar Allan Poe. I tear over to Westlunds' and borrow two eggs for Mom but just Mrs. Westlund is there, or she's the only one I see. Then Bud and I try the radio but too much static. Usually we can get WCCO from Minneapolis fine, but not with a storm coming.

And the afternoon's just about done. It's really snowing now. Tiny flakes going crosswise that hit like pinpricks in the face, almost like frozen sand. There'll be drifts in the morning.

"Ray, do close the *door,*" Mom says. She's almost finished getting things ready for the potluck. Now all we have to do is get cleaned up and wait.

# 3

It's only three blocks to Grace Methodist Church where we go. The other four are all Lutheran. And a Baptist, I almost forgot. Dad leads the way down the middle of the street between the ruts so we can see better in the dark and the blowing snow. No cars out anyway. Then comes Mom, carrying the angel food. Then me, carrying our dishes and silverware and cups in a picnic basket and dragging Bud.

"He's drunk, Ray. Dad's drunk." Bud knows Dad can't hear him in the wind.

I turn and walk backwards a few steps, facing Bud. "Not really. Just a little tight, but it'll be okay. Come on now."

He did have a few snorts down at the store, no question. But he's not bad. He usually has a few snorts on potluck supper nights. Other nights, too.

Everybody zooms right into the church basement where it's warm. Hot, in fact. Like going from an icehouse into a blast furnace. We hang up our coats and things and there's the usual chatter all over the place. Mom heads for the big kitchen with the angel food and some of the ladies. Smells like coffee.

And baked beans.

In the big Sunday School room where we have the supper, the partitions are pushed back and the folding tables and chairs are set up and the long table already has food on it—the serving table that's planks on sawhorses with white paper on top. Reverend Parker meets us, rubbing his hands. He's always cold, or acts like it.

"Well, well, the Deckers. Frank, you're looking fit! What a night, eh? Raymond, Jefferson, you boys all set to put on the feed bag?"

He smiles, but his face is so thin that it doesn't look right. He smiles because it's potluck-supper night but I don't think he's really all that happy about it. Benson said he looks like a scarecrow in the full moon at midnight, which wasn't too nice to say probably, but comes pretty close. He's seventy-three years old, is how old he is, and absent-minded to boot.

But he lays the law down, you've got to admit that. He's darn near as strict as Reverend Fredrickson at Bethel Lutheran, but not quite. I mean to tell you, that's Missouri Synod and you can't dance or go to the movies or hardly breathe.

He pats us on the head and laughs like a maniac. He always does at these suppers and church picnics. I'm not wild about potluck suppers, like I say, but there *is* plenty of food and—

"You boys behave yourselves now!" Dad shouts so loud that other people turn and stare. "Ray, see to it that Bud has a good time!" He could have said that before we got here. Or not at all. Then he goes through the crowd to rave about the food. He always does, which I guess is all right. "Mrs. Antonsen, save me a wedge of that pie of yours. . . . Mrs. Beck, those meatballs, you've done it again. . . . My favorite tuna hot dish, Mrs. Drexel, I'll enjoy it to the hilt. . . ."

I look around. There's Foster and Savre. They're both *seniors*. Coming this way, back into the hall a little. They walk right into us, smiling, and shove me and Bud back into the hanging coats, against the hooks.

"Hey, Decker," Savre says, trying to imitate my father. "Take care of little Bud now, like a good boy, huh?" They laugh, damn them. Bud kicks Savre in the shin and I grab Bud. Savre lets out a yell. *"You little . . ."* People look around and he rubs his shin and lets up on us. He smiles for the crowd and rubs Bud's hair and whispers, "I'll get you for that, you little fart."

There's Benson. Good. I drag Bud and we push through the people. Benson's sitting on a folding chair turned backwards. He's a good guy to see.

"Hey Benson."

"Hey Deck, how's it going? Hiya, Bud. Savre push you around, did he?"

"Yah."

"Me too. Forget it. They got solid muscle where their brains ought to be."

Hammer slides out of his mother's arm around his shoulder and comes over.

"Hey Deck. Hey Benson."

"Hey Hammer, what's up?"

"Nothing. Gladys is here, Decker."

"So?"

"Just thought you'd want to know," and he snickers.

He's not a bad guy but he's always poking around. Wears glasses and thinks it's smart to tear around with big news like "Gladys is here." Jeez, I saw her the minute we came into the room, but I didn't run around like a dope telling everybody.

Now the room's jammed with people and the food's all out on the long table. Hot dishes, including Mrs. Parmer's chili that you don't take if you know what's good for you, salads with marshmallows, rolls and pickles, desserts, coffee for grownups, cocoa for the kids. You get to know what's going to show up at these things. And everything's a little loose and when you pile it on your plate it runs together. Bud keeps his stuff separate even if he has to put his fingers between the helpings.

Deacon Beeker gets the nod from Reverend Parker and he leaves off inspecting the Sunday School work tacked up on the folded partitions. He usually knocks a partition over but not tonight.

"Friends, brothers and sisters," he yells, "and *little* brothers and sisters." This is a joke. Every time. Every blessed time, he throws that in and expects the kids to roll on the floor laughing. He's about a hundred years old, all wrinkled up, with a gimpy leg he's proud of because he was run over by a state senator's carriage in 1902 or something. I can't stand him.

"It's time we partake of this bountiful board, with the Lord's blessing. Children first now. 'Suffer little children,' you know."

Another joke.

So Savre and some of the older kids start through the line with their plates and the rest of us hang around and grownups push us into line. I push Bud ahead of me and he whispers, "I'm going to throw up."

"No you won't."

"Yes I will; you wait."

He probably will, that's the sad truth of the matter. He usually does, from the excitement and stuffy room. Maybe not this time.

Anyway, we get through the line. This means we've got to sit and stare at our plates while everything runs together and gets cold, until *everybody* is at the tables except four or five ladies in the kitchen, including Mom, to make coffee and bring out more tuna hot dishes.

"Let us *pray!*"

We all stand behind our folding chairs and bow while Reverend Parker keeps banging a water glass with his spoon. Someone tells the ladies in the kitchen to be quiet, Reverend Parker finally stops banging the fool glass, and away he goes.

"Dear God, receive our thanks for this bountiful repast we are about to . . . about to engage in . . . eating. For we are your *hum*ble servants gathered together in this your *holy* house. . . ."

Benson looks cross-eyed at me, and Bud snorts. We bow lower and Bud's shaking but he's quiet.

"We know we have sinned in thine eyes, O Lord, and we ask your for*give*ness. Keep the storm outside in . . . keep the . . . *protect* us from the storm while we pause to remember those dear departed whom you saw fit to lift up to your heavenly home for everlasting glory. Comfort, uh . . . *com*fort those in need everywhere, those who see the light before they, too, are called. Teach us to toil in thy vineyards here on earth as we . . . in thy name we . . . *Lord,* in thy name we ask for*give*ness and bless this food to our use, in the name of the Father and the Son and the Holy Ghost. Amen."

Reverend Parker's really best at funerals. No kidding. He does a bang-up job, especially at the graveside. Now we shuffle into our chairs and dig into the food even though the Jell-O's runny and the gravy's stiff on the meatballs. But it's a sin to leave food on your plate in these hard times with all the starving children in China, anybody will tell you that.

Bud's sitting beside me, and Gladys happens to be across from me sitting next to Irene Foley, who happens to be a real deadbeat. We all sit at the same table; I mean no grownups.

"Hi, Ray and Bud," Gladys says. She's got her hair in curls and she's wearing a keen sweater. You can tell, too. I mean even without the curls, she's sure no boy, let me tell you. I keep thinking of the pink kimono.

"Hiya, Gladys. Your dad get the car fixed?"

She smiles and nods her head and Irene giggles and spills baked beans off her fork. I hate girls who giggle. She's sort of a female Hammer.

So we plow through our food. Jeez, it's hot. The room, I mean. Close your eyes and you can hear all the chatter and the silverware clattering on the dishes and chairs scraping on the linoleum when people go back for seconds.

"I got to go," Bud whispers, pulling me down by the shirt sleeve.

"To the toilet?"

"Yah. Now."

"Well, go ahead. You know where it is."

"You got to come, Ray. I got to throw up."

He does look pretty white, so we push our chairs back and I throw in "Excuse me" for any grownup watching. In the toilet off the hallway by the furnace room, it's cold, I don't know why. And Bud throws up like anything. I hold him around the waist.

"There, better? Splash some water on your face."

I pull the chain but the old toilet doesn't work right and the puke just floats around. For a minute

I figure it's going to overflow, but it doesn't. I'm not too happy about this whole thing myself; feel a little queasy. I splash some water on my face, too, and it's like ice. We wipe our hands on the roller towel and Bud says, "I'm going home. You going home, Ray? Let's go home."

"We can't, ya dummy. You know that."

But then I hear Mrs. Semple, my piano teacher, bashing out some chords on the old Sunday School piano that's needed tuning since the *Titanic* went down. They're pushing chairs around and getting ready for community singing. I figure what the heck, nobody will miss us. I don't mean going *home,* but I take Bud and we go up the back stairway into the cold sanctuary where Reverend Parker preaches every Sunday except when he's laid up with rheumatism, and then Deacon Beeker preaches, which is worse.

"What are we up here for?" Bud whispers. We sit down in the back pew.

"I don't know. Just until you feel better."

Me too, but I don't say this. It's quiet. I can hear them singing "What a Friend We Have in Jesus" downstairs but it's like listening with earmuffs on. And I hear the wind up here. Pretty soon we can see things in the dark, even see the blizzard through the windows, not the stained-glass ones. It's nice here, but we sure shouldn't *be* here in the sanctuary. It's just not done except on Sundays or funerals. I mean if anybody knew, we—

"Someone's coming!"

Bud scrunches down in the pew. He's right. Soft footsteps. Gladys! She stops about ten feet from where we are and we keep quiet. Then when she can see better, she waves and comes over and sits right down and leans against me! Bud slides off the pew onto the floor.

"Hi, Ray. Bud, are you all right?" she whispers.

"He's okay, Glad. We just came up for a minute, but jeezus, you shouldn't be here!"

The sanctuary is Reverend Parker's territory, which he shares with God, and nobody's allowed in on a Saturday *night,* of all things. *She* knows that!

"Don't say that in church, silly."

"Say what?"

"You know," and she laughs and leans against me harder. It *is* cold. "Ray, do your folks let you skate on Sunday? Mine do."

I'm getting dizzy again. She talks just like there's nothing wrong, but my God, my gosh, if anybody—

"Somebody's coming!" Bud whispers again. He sits up fast to get a look and cracks his head on the hymnal holder.

*"Damn!"* he shouts. And the lights go on!

Just like that, lights! There's the Reverend at the switch and old man Westlund and Dad! They stand like statues, looking right at us and not saying a word for a coon's age.

Bud scrambles out and Dad grabs him by the arm. Gladys shakes her head off my shoulder and

31

walks to her father with a swing to her hips, but she's scared. Has to be. I stand up and crack my knee on the pew in front.

"Bud didn't feel good, so . . ."

"Raymond," the Reverend says. He lets out a loud sigh that sounds like the wind outside. "Raymond, this is not what I expected of *you*, of all people, not at all. And in God's holy house. You're going to tell us that Alice—"

"Gladys."

"That Gladys here was sick, too?"

"She came up later," Bud says, squirming. But Dad holds on. I hope Bud doesn't kick him. "Came up by herself. Tell 'em, Gladys!"

"Gladys and Bud and I weren't doing anything wrong. Bud threw up, and—"

"Raymond, this is disgraceful," my father says. "Absolutely disgraceful. Now you get yourself down there and take Bud along. The very idea! *March,* young man!"

In front of Gladys, jeez. She doesn't say anything, damn her. Well, what can she say, I suppose. Nobody would believe her anyway, or me either. Still . . . And all the time her old man says nothing, just looks at me like I'm a fly in his farina or something.

The Reverend slowly checks the doors and turns off the lights. They're swinging into "Onward, Christian Soldiers" downstairs and it's crazy, but I have to march in time, I can't help it. At the bottom of the stairs Dad whirls and slams me into the coats the way Savre did, only not as hard. He still smells like a few snorts of booze.

"Now you get your wraps on and get Bud ready, and I mean *now,* mister smart aleck."

He says it through his teeth like James Cagney and he's sweating like a horse, but he doesn't look me in the eye. He follows old man Westlund and Gladys into the Sunday School room and he's back in a flash, grunting with his coat and overshoes. He never puts his overshoes on first. It's easier, but he doesn't because I told him about it last winter and he didn't appreciate that.

Out in the blizzard, he loses his steam, with just the three of us. "Your mother's helping clean up," he yells. "We're heading home and I'm just going to consider this matter closed, Raymond. I can't understand what gets into you. What will our friends think? Honest to God, sinful behavior is . . . Well, we just can't have it, you hear? What kind of example is that for Bud!"

"But Dad," I yell into the wind, "all we did was, Bud got sick and I—"

"Shut up! Just shut your trap! Tomorrow at church, you pay attention, understand? Lying and sin and fooling around with young girls and . . ." His voice is carried off by a blast of wind, a real roar.

"*You* going?" Bud shouts.

"That's enough out of *you*. *Ray's* going, that's for sure."

The bastard. He won't be in church. He never is on Sunday. And nobody listens. Nobody. My throat's tight like I swallowed lemon juice and my God I'm crying! Just a little. Nobody will know though. *Nobody*. In a blizzard—even a small one like tonight—you always come in with tears on your face. Mom will, too, when she gets home with the picnic basket and the cake tin. Not even Bud will know. Boy, things turn upside down in a hurry if you're a kid. Damn them all!

Dad pours himself a nightcap when we get in—half a water glass of whiskey—and sends us up to bed. Up in our attic room it's great under the quilts with the storm swishing around the house. Things start to settle down in my stomach.

"Ray," Bud says from his bunk bed, in the dark.

"Yah."

"Why'd they get so mad? Jeez, all we did was—"

"Nothing. Forget it." I don't feel like telling him what they were thinking about me and Gladys, but they were thinking the worst, you can count on that. They always do. Probably figured we were messing around with Gladys's virginity, right there in the church. And she'd have a baby out of wedlock. And we'd both be damned forever, and what would that look like for the families. I mean sometimes parents and preachers act that way, at least those I know. And Gladys didn't say a *word*. Maybe later she did. Maybe she is right now.

"Ray."

*"Yah."*

"I did have to throw up, honest."

"I know, Bud. G'night."

# 4

After all the hubbub, nothing much happened because of the potluck business. Nothing I didn't expect anyway. Dad snorted around like a penned bull for a while and spouted about responsibility till it was coming out his ears. Mom was on her high horse, too; I didn't look for that. And Gladys didn't say anything for a few days, even at school. I stayed mad, but things settled down and I don't feel like clobbering anyone now.

Today's the first Friday in March and it's pretty warm, for March. Fridays I don't have much spare time. I've got the piano lesson and I clean up the store. The way it works is, I come home for dinner at noon and pick up the music and the money and stop at Mrs. Semple's for the piano lesson after school. Then I stop by home and change and then down to the store.

I got the money this noon—thirty-five cents per lesson and hard to come by. Dad reminds me every time and so does Mom, but not *every* time. So I swing by Mrs. Semple's. She's been teaching piano since the ice age, but she's okay. Always says something like "That's fine, just fine, Raymond. But remember. Keep your wrists high. We don't want the wrists to fall."

"Okay, Mrs. Semple. Here's the money."

"Thank you, dear."

She's a big woman, really big, with sort of red hair most of the time and she must eat a lot of onions or something. She puts the money in an old cigar box on her end table.

"Now you know what to work on for next time."

"Oh, yes. Yah, no problem."

She takes her glasses off, the kind that don't have anything to go over your ears, and says, "Now say hello to your folks for me like a good boy."

So I promise her I will and the next pupil is tromping in as I put my jacket on and leave. I *am* doing well, I know that, but it's no big deal. That sounds like a lot of hooey, but what I mean is I like it and it comes easy, all kinds of music. It's like Benson can chase down a fly ball with his eyes closed and put it away every time. Or Kernes can clear four hockey boards at the skating rink. They work at it, sure, but it comes easy, too. I tripped just trying to clear two boards last week. Might be my skates need sharpening. And in the summer I'm lucky to get a glove on most fly balls. Sun gets in my eyes. Or dust.

So it's no big deal, the piano. It's just something I do, like walking home to change. Some of the snow's melting, but it'll freeze solid and jagged again tonight. When I get to the house and go in the front door, nobody says anything. There's some-body home though. You can tell. You can always tell.

"Mom, I'm home."

A chair moves in the dining room and I can hear Bud up in our attic room, bouncing his butt on the floor. He says it toughens his stomach muscles, don't ask me why.

"Ray, we're in the dining room," Mom says. "How did the lesson go?"

"Fine."

We? Who's we?

Dad's there. At four in the afternoon!

"Dad? What are you . . . Why aren't you at the store? You okay or what?"

He just sits there and flips his spectacles back and forth on the table. So I sit down and drink a glass of milk and eat a couple of store-bought cookies.

"Your father wants to talk to you, Ray. How was school?"

"Okay."

As a matter of fact, it was a pretty rotten day in a lot of ways but not the kind of thing you talk over with your parents. And the weekend's coming up anyway.

I wait, but he just sits there with the late after-noon sunlight showing where he combs his hair over to hide the bald. He sighs like the Reverend and keeps fiddling with his spectacles.

"Bud's up in our room, huh."

"Yes, he is," Mom answers. She pours a cup of coffee for my father and stands there with the coffeepot. "That's what your father wants to talk to you about, Ray. That's why he's home."

"Bud? He's okay, or what? I'll go up and—"

"You'll do nothing of the sort, Raymond. You'll sit right here until we have this thing out."

So my father talks. A miracle! Even if he does talk into his coffee cup. He's good at this waiting game and it usually works, I have to admit. I mean I sit and try to figure. Bud's sick? Sassed the teacher? Skipped school? No, I saw him there. And what the heck has it got to do with *me?* I'm getting better at it, at the waiting.

"Ray, your father's really upset about Bud."

"Oh."

And I wait. And wait.

"That's right," he finally says. "That's right, I *am,* and with good reason."

He wipes the back of his hand across his forehead and drums his fingers on the table to show how upset he is.

"So what's Bud done? What's the problem?"

"Ray, your father thinks that Bud stole money from the store."

He looks up at her. She's still holding the coffeepot.

"I don't *think,* Laura. I *know.* I was there, don't forget, and I saw with my own eyes. And Raymond,

I'm not happy, not happy at all with the way you handled this."

"I *know* you were there, Frank," Mom says.

Aw jeez, what now. It wasn't *that* bad a day.

"Dad, I don't get it. Honest, I just don't get it. Bud wouldn't . . . *You* know Bud wouldn't take money from the store. He just wouldn't! And what did *I* have to—"

"*Raymond!*"

My father almost squeals. He puts on his spectacles and his coat and jams his hat on his head and trots out the front door. On the way he says, "Raymond, I want you two to get this all straightened out, you hear? And now!"

"But what did I—"

The door bangs shut. Another bang from the kitchen when Mom puts the coffeepot back on the range.

"Mom, what's Dad talking about? I mean what happened?"

She sits down at the table, holding both her elbows. No smiles but at least she'll tell me.

"Ray, your father says Bud went down to the store after school and took two dollars from the cash register. Dad stopped him on the way out and brought him home, but Bud wouldn't talk. Just ran up to the attic room. He did say you gave him the idea. And that's all I know."

"But I didn't have anything to do with this. Good gosh, neither did Bud, I'll bet, whatever it is. Do *you* think he stole the money, *do* you?"

"No, no, it's not like Bud at all, but your father says—"

"Well then why didn't you . . . How come we have to go through all this crazy talk with Dad, huh? I just don't get it."

She looks at me and then takes a big sigh and looks out the window.

"Ray, I'll tell you something about your father and you'll understand."

"Yah?"

"He drinks."

"Well, I know that, but why does he get so—"

"You don't remember how bad it was when he used to drink so much, you just don't remember."

"But he doesn't drink a lot, no more than a lot of men in town. Still he keeps getting all het up over—"

"And . . . *and,* he cannot leave women . . . that is, our marriage is a holy wedlock but that's not enough for him and never has been, you understand?"

"I guess so."

She stands up and pours herself a cup of coffee.

"And he cannot manage a paper route, much less a store. If I hadn't taken over running that store—"

"But Dad and Agnes work."

"Ray, I keep the books, I hired Agnes, I told your father what to do and what not to do. Otherwise we would have lost it sure as you're born, just like old Mr. Ferris lost it to us in '32. Well, that's the truth of the matter."

"Mom, all that may be true but—"

"It is."

"Okay, but why does he take after *us* all the time? That's what I don't understand."

"You boys?"

"Yah, me and Bud."

"Oh, to prove he's a big man, I guess, a proper father, and a breadwinner, I don't know. I've given up trying to figure it all out, but it won't last, Ray. Believe me, it won't last."

"Why not?"

"Because you won't let it. You won't, and that's a fact. Now, can you talk to Bud?"

"Yah, I suppose. But I can't see how things are going to change, I really can't."

I go to the bathroom and splash some water on my face, rub hard with the hand towel. I feel a little queasy. Jeez. Take the narrow steps two at a time, duck the head, round the corner, and I'm in our attic room. It cost Dad almost one hundred dollars to have Ben Watson finish it off. Don't know why I thought of that except I've heard it a hundred times. But it is nice. And now Dad can say he has a study—our old room downstairs where Mom keeps the books for the store. She works on them Sunday nights.

Bud's sitting on the rug, wrapped up in his quilt

so just the top of his head shows.

"Hey Bud."

"Ummp."

I take off my school clothes and get into my over-all pants and sweat shirt. I sit on the edge of the bed to change shoes and Bud doesn't move.

"Bud."

"Ummp."

"Bud, you'll smother in there."

I want to get this over with, I really do, but it saves time if I don't rush it. In the long run, that is.

"Hiya!"

He throws off the quilt and he's all smiles. His eyes are puffed up though. He's been crying.

"Look."

He holds up two dollar bills, one of them torn partway. I suppose he wouldn't give them up. That's a lot of dough.

"Ray, see this? This torn one? They'll be after me, you wait. It's a federal offense."

"What're you talking about?"

He stuffs the bills in his pocket.

"To rip a dollar bill. It is. G-men come after you and they track you down and it doesn't matter how far you go or how good you hide or growing a beard or anything, they find you and the old Tommy guns come out and—"

"Bud, for Pete's sake. Dad's got this story about you stealing some—"

"Dad's full of shit."

No smiles now. Back to the old Sitting Bull. I don't know where he gets that language but I don't feel like arguing about it now.

"Come on, what went on? What happened? He thinks we cooked up something together and I don't even know what the heck went on!"

"You'll tell."

"No I won't. Tell who?"

"The G-men!"

He grins and pulls the quilt over again. The fathead. He'll come around. He waits a few secs, then tosses the quilt off and scrunches around on his butt so he's facing me.

"I went to the store after school."

"Yah?"

"And I said hello to Dad like he wants, and Agnes was waiting on somebody."

Agnes works for Dad. I didn't know Mom hired her before. She's a spinster lady about thirty, I guess, or a little younger. She really does most of the work while he drinks coffee with the gang at the restaurant or stands around looking busy. Been with him quite a while, she has. She's nice.

"So? You said hello, and then?"

"And I put eight quarters in the drawer in the register. That's right for two dollar bills, isn't it? Eight?"

"Yah, sure, you know that. And then?"

"And then Dad turns up and grabs my arm and says he caught me and drags me home and tells

44

Mom I stole two dollars, that's all. Oh, and he doesn't want to hear another word out of me, so I shut up. And you know what I'm going to do when I grow up, Ray?"

I'm still trying to figure this out and I barely hear the last part.

"Do you, Ray?"

"No, what?"

"I'm going to bash him. *Bam!*" He slams his fist into the side of the bed. I know it hurts but he doesn't flinch. He's tough.

"You can't do that, Bud. You can't just go around—"

"No, not *now,* I'm too small. When I grow *up.* Then I'll—"

"Okay, okay!"

I grab his fist because he's going to do it again. Then I drop it.

"Bud, I still can't figure out . . ."

"Don't you believe me, Ray?"

"Oh come on. I told them *downstairs* that you wouldn't do that. But what's Dad getting at? Why does he think we were in this together or something?"

"Oh, yah. I told him you gave me the idea and then he got mad so I shut up. I know. I'll cut his suspenders and pour cement in his shoes when he's asleep."

"I gave you the idea? Bud, shut up now. *I* gave you the idea? When?"

"When you said I better not mail the quarters."

Well, I'm a fool. An honest-to-God solid-gold moron. I remember now. Bud showed me his quarters last week. That's two months of allowance. And the advertisement out of *Popular Mechanics* for this detective outfit with fingerprint stuff and all, for $1.99. And for that money it should be almost professional stuff.

I finish tying my shoes.

"Okay, Bud, that's what I didn't know, see. I forgot. You going to send away for it now?"

"Nope."

"*No.* Why not?"

"I don't *have* to. I'm going to stash it away where nobody will ever find it, see. The money's *mine.*"

"Yah, sure it is, but—"

"I'll tell *you* the hiding place in case they get me, see, so you can come back later and—"

"Oh, come on, Bud. Look, I'll tell Dad what went on and maybe he'll understand."

"No he won't. Forget it."

And he's right. He won't.

"What about Mom, Bud? We could tell her and she could—"

"Naw, let's not tell anybody, just you."

Darn it all, he *is* making sense, too. Okay, so we leave it a secret between me and Bud. Mom doesn't think he took the money. Maybe sometime she'll tell *him* that.

# 5

Boy, it's getting warm now, even in late afternoon, and the snow's mostly gone. Just slush except in the shady corners and the alleys. But you never know about April.

I cut across the muddy churchyard and past the creamery where every second grade class goes to watch them pasteurize milk and make cottage cheese and butter. Then into the alley by the bank. It's the backside of Main Street. Part of it, anyway. Main Street curves along the river, so the alley does, too. I like it back here; not everybody does.

"Hey, Master Decker. Friday cleanup at the establishment?"

That's Irv, the back-shop man at the *Weekly Herald*. He does everything—sets type, puts the pages together, reads to see there are no mistakes, runs the press on Wednesdays. Now he sits on the back steps of the shop and takes a break and smokes a roll-your-own.

"That's right. How ya doing?"

"I at this moment have the world by the tail, my friend. Few souls in the community realize this."

And he winks.

Funny, I used to be scared of Irv, I don't know why. He goes his own way. Dad calls him a tramp, but not to his face. Oh, we've got tramps all right, in the summertime anyway. From all over.

Hobos ride the freights and sometimes jump off or climb on when the trains slow down on the long hill out of the valley. The railroad guys don't give them much trouble out here, but I guess they still do in Minneapolis and Chicago.

Yah, there's kind of a shantytown over there in the cottonwoods and sumac between the tracks and the river—some pretty swell places to bed down, made of old cartons and crates, old corrugated iron, barrels, snow fence, almost anything. Some of the hobos stay just overnight to stretch their bones and others stay for a week or two and go around town trying to mow a lawn or do odd jobs around the house—anything for a meal.

Benson and I got to know two of them last summer. Myron and the Preacher. That's all they were called. Myron and the Preacher. Myron was an English teacher from Detroit, Michigan, and the Preacher was a minister from Lexington, Kentucky. I loved the way he talked. He said, "No, come on now, it's not 'you-all,' it's 'yawl,' like one word, y'hear?" They and some other fellas threw all their food together in a pot—some corn, a can of beans and bacon, some string beans and carrots from a garden, a soup bone—and they invited us to try it.

Pretty good, really. Preacher said, "Yawl remember now, we jes' borrowed the beans an' the carrots."

Oh, there's some pretty shifty guys, too, from time to time, and a fight or two every week, but nobody hardly ever gets hurt. I wouldn't say they were a bad lot, like Dad does. He's never been there. He just says that they're tramps and should get out and get work, but that's what they're trying to do. Most of them, anyway. They're mostly heading West. It must be getting pretty crowded in California.

But Irv, he's been here as long as I can remember. He's maybe almost as old as Dad and I still call him Irv. You get to know people in the alley.

He takes a careful swig of booze from his half pint and puts it back in his denim apron pocket.

"To your health, Master Decker."

"Yah, Irv. Well, I better be going."

"Correct, my friend. Up the rungs of the ladder of success while I . . ." He fades off.

"While you what?"

"While I sit here up to my ass in social notes, you should pardon my early English. Ten hours of setting social notes and every name spelled absolutely correctly. *Absolutely*. Solutely. Salute, my friend."

And he waves me on. He's a little pie-eyed, but everybody expects this. He's never mean when he boozes and even half-crocked he's the best back-shop man in this part of the state, maybe the *whole* state. If he wasn't a back-shop printer and didn't drink, he'd be a gentleman probably. He sure talks like one.

Pete, the blacksmith, is clanging away. A lot of his trade is with car owners now, but he still does a fair amount of machinery for the farmers—broken plowshares, harness hardware, that kind of thing. I love to watch him; so do all the guys, and he doesn't mind as long as you stand back. He sees me and waves his big hammer and I wave. Can't hear very well. And tough? Wow.

The paper and the blacksmith shop are across the alley, not with front doors facing Main Street. Then there's Dave's shoe repair that smells good, and Sam's junkyard down at the end. What a place that junkyard is. A guy can spend hours just looking around at old auto parts, barrel hoops, boxes of hinges, old fancy mirrors, good kerosene lamps, old farm tools, more than I can think of even. We always go there for wheels if we're building a push-mobile or something. Even Sam doesn't know what all he's got.

On our side of the alley, the River Café is next door to the dime store. The kitchen door's open and the smell of onion gravy and meat loaf and vinegar is enough to knock you for a loop. Mr. Schweitzer owns it and does the cooking. He stands outside in the shadows, cooling off. A big fat guy.

"Young Decker," he says, "you tell that father of yours to keep his trash cans over *there,* not over *here*. You see? There's his place, here's my place, he should sometimes understand. You understand, do you?"

"I'll tell him."

Mr. Schweitzer never smiles that I know of, but it's kind of hard to tell with that bushy mustache. Course it stays hot in that kitchen, winter or summer. Nothing to smile about. But we get along fine. Sometimes he asks me in and we sit at a little table in the restaurant kitchen and have iced tea. I'd do it oftener only I really can't take that smell. I mean I really can't, no offense. Makes me sick to my stomach. And the cats I don't particularly like. Seven of them and all good mousers.

"Halloo, the good doctor!"

Irv's shouting down the alley. He keeps calling Mr. Schweitzer "the doctor," I don't know why.

"In the flesh, Irv, and not a thing in the world on my conscience, *nothing*. I sleep well at night, like a baby I sleep."

"And why not? A noble upstanding figure of a man. A saint among sinners, full of the milk of human kindness. And sausage. And beer."

Irv really slings the words around. They both do. Mr. Schweitzer wipes his red hands on his greasy apron and turns to go in. I love to listen to them go at it even if I don't understand it all.

"Irv, Irv, you talk too much, and say not enough. Away from the bottle and then converse, eh?"

Irv starts back into the shop to finish up.

"Just a precaution, good sir, a medicinal preventive."

"Yeah? For what, I may ask?"

"For me, so I can partake of that savory meat loaf tonight and live to see another day!" Irv shouts and waves as he disappears into the shop.

"Bah. Drunken fool. Decker, he's a madman, pay no attention. And tell your father—"

"I will, I will. Got to run now."

They go at it six days a week. Maybe seven; I don't know where Irv is on Sundays.

Here's the back door of the dime store. Needs paint, the store does, but they all do, except the brick ones. I hop the three wooden steps and shove the door open with my shoulder. I've got my piano book because I came straight from Mrs. Semple's this time, so I toss it on the scruffy old sofa.

The back room is a catchall. There's one light hanging down in the middle of the small room, and I pull the cord on. Dad's desk is a pile of old papers and dirty coffee cups and glasses. Along one side there's the shelves for the extra stock—carpet tacks, coat thread, darning needles, penholders, blotters, phony necklaces, all sorts of merchandise. Labels on the wood shelves say what goes where but nobody's used them right for years. I just sort of remember where things are, or hunt them down, or ask Agnes. She doesn't forget a thing, and she's nice about telling a person. I think she's a little shy, but that's fine with me and customers sure like her. I don't think that she has any family.

On the other side are the narrow steps down to the cellar and furnace room where the cleaning stuff is. The main part of the store you can't see from back here because the green drapes are pulled shut.

"Ray, that you?"

Dad's coming into the back room. We have to talk over what needs to be done and see if there's anything special.

"Yah, Dad. Mr. Schweitzer says you should keep your trash cans away from his place."

Dad flips the drapes aside and sits on a corner of the desk in his shirt sleeves with the little rubber bands holding his cuffs up so they don't get dirty. Now he's not exactly overjoyed to see me.

"What's that?"

"Mr. Schweitzer says you should keep your—"

"All right, Raymond, you can tell that over-stuffed Kraut that he can damn well mind his own business. I buy plenty of coffee over there and he knows it."

I just nod. Dad does that. Tells me to tell somebody else. He may not know it, but I'm not about to tell Mr. Schweitzer what he said or what he called him. We're Krauts too, come to think of it.

"So I'll check the stock first? See what's low out front?"

"Check the front stock. Of *course* check first and see what's low. Agnes will . . . I told Agnes what

I need, so you just ask her. You're late, aren't you."

"No."

"Well don't be."

And he goes into the toilet behind his desk. There's a couple of *Police Gazette*s in there. I've seen them. And always a bottle of whiskey stashed up high on top of the flush box. I've seen that, too.

Out front it's nicer. Neater. Agnes is up at the cash register with her gray sweater on and the pencil stuck in her hair. Two or three women are waiting for her to wait on them, so I walk up the left aisle, wave at Agnes, and go out the front door with the awning crank. I don't know why he had the awning down today, but never mind, it's fun cranking it up. Starting to get dark. It'll freeze tonight, sure as you're born.

Half an hour to closing. I wait for Agnes to get a break and there's Mrs. Westlund buying some thread and measuring spoons. Agnes rings up twenty cents with a thank you and Mrs. Westlund almost bumps into me. She's in a hurry.

"Ray! Excuse me."

"My fault."

"I really have to run. Why don't we see you these days? You stop by now. I know Gladys would like to see you."

How about *that*. Gladys hasn't said much except just, well, I mean about *us*. Maybe old man Westlund's cooled off now. Maybe . . .

"Raymond, will you get a move on!" Dad shouts

from the back of the store. He comes up front, putting on his suit coat and buttoning his vest. "Lovely day," he says with a smile when he sees one more customer. I don't know her and she says "Yes, indeed," and leaves. Agnes knows her.

Dad stands with his hands behind his back and looks out the front window. I get Agnes aside.

"Well," she says, "it's not bad, Ray. Take a look around, but mainly the school supplies. I know we're low there. And the light bulbs."

She goes back to figuring up the cash and I take a look at the cupboards under the school-supplies counter. Low, all right. And light bulbs. Agnes doesn't make mistakes. I look under all the counters on my way back and see I need to bring up some shoelaces, too.

So back to the storeroom, climb up on the stool, find the right stuff. Lucky this time. I bring it out and stock the cupboards under the counters, so Agnes won't run out tomorrow night when the farmers come in. During the week, it's mainly the men coming in once in a while to bring in a harness for fixing or pick up some chicken mash at the feed mill.

But on Saturday night the whole families come in and the kids go to the movies if they're lucky. Stores stay open until ten o'clock. The farm women, some of them, take eggs in, either at the creamery or one of the grocery stores for cash, and pick up what they need, like baking powder or coffee.

In good weather, everybody stands around, the men do—town men, too—with one foot on the bumper of cars parked on Main Street, and they laugh and argue and just talk, lots of times in Norwegian or Swedish. I can't tell the difference, but don't let them hear you say *that*. There's no love lost between the Norskis and the Svenskis.

Oh, I like Saturday nights. They all laugh about the crops or the weather that they've been moaning about all week. Most of them do. But it's the busiest time of the week in the dime store, so I don't want Agnes to have to go back for supplies. Dad even helps on Saturday night.

Well, then down to the cellar with a flashlight to get the oil mop and the special sawdust. This part is fun. Sprinkle the special sawdust on the wood floor, all over the store, start at the front and sweep it all back. The wood floor really does smarten up and look good. Then sweep the dirty sawdust into a box and put the cleaning stuff back down in the cellar. I don't use the oil mop this time. Only every other Friday and I did it last Friday, I forgot. Go over the clean floor with *that* and it *really* looks great.

And *then* the burning. I balance empty cartons and trash, grab a wooden match from a tin box on the wall, and go out into the alley. It's still partly light, but not for long. Put the cartons in the old steel barrel along with the other junk stacked out back, especially any excelsior, and light it. Little black shreds float up and the barrel settles a little in the ice when it gets hot, but I keep a watch on it and there's Savre.

There's Savre! Just cutting through, won't see me. He's not looking for me. Big-deal letter sweater. He's just going home and just happens to be—

"Decker, hey, a big boy now. Helping Daddy run the store, ain't that cute?"

He leans against the telephone pole right in front of the barrel and spits. It misses my foot and sizzles on the hot barrel. He grins. Nobody else in the alley. Not that I can see. God.

"Hi, Savre."

Damn, my voice shakes. I'm acting like a kid, sounding like a kid. Whooo, boy.

"Where's your kid brother, Raymond, the little one that should have his ass kicked around the block, huh? He leave you all unprotected? Huh!"

He jabs me hard in the chest.

"He's home."

But I'm coughing, trying to get my wind.

"And you're down here helping Daddy like a good boy, right?"

He grabs a fistful of my hair and jerks. Jeezus!

"Is that *right,* I said!"

"Savre, lay off!"

Can't stop now, can't go. Kick him hard in the crotch. He screams, bends over. White face, lashes out with his left arm. Catches me on the cheek with his class ring. Feel it tear. God! Kneels down, grabs a smoking stick, takes a big breath—

"Well, now step right up, ladies and gentlemen!"

It's Irv. He's standing right over Savre and shouting like a carnival barker. But the alley's empty.

"Step right up, I say, and observe this primate throwback, this unholy ass-backwards mutation, young Savre by name!"

Savre's so mad he can't talk. He trembles. He's big—God, he's big. Irv smiles at him, takes a nip from the half pint, and throws his arms out wide like somebody acting Shakespeare.

"Young Savre by name and child beater by fame. Correct, my fine young swain? One of our finest, and I, *I* know whereof I speak because I am up to my ass in social notes. Savre, ladies and gentlemen, is a social note of the first water!"

Irv suddenly stops and just looks at Savre. They look at each other. Then so fast I can't believe it, he grabs Savre by the letter sweater, slams him against the telephone pole, and throws him down the alley. Savre doesn't lose his footing, but he has to really stagger. And he moves off, fast. Doesn't even shout back. Irv sits down on the steps.

"Just to catch my breath, Master Decker."

"Irv, I—"

"You were doing nicely, very nicely. It just so happened that you were grossly outgunned. I do enjoy a fair encounter, but you would have been a mess. Can't have messes in our alley. I'll say good evening to you."

He gets up and Dad blasts through the back door.

"Ray, what's going on? Who's that? Irv?"

"At your service."

"You better move it along, Irv, we've got to think of the influence on the boy here."

Irv stands, weaves a little, and smiles at my father. He lifts his chin high and says, "Frank Decker, you, as always, are absolutely right. As always. I shall—"

"Now wait. I didn't—"

"I shall take my leave of you both." And he goes into Mr. Schweitzer's kitchen.

Dad doesn't see the blood on my face; just as well. It's right on the cheekbone so it doesn't bleed much, but sting! Jeez! He looks around and finds the stick Savre was going to use. He tosses it into the barrel.

"Got to keep an eye on these, Ray. Do it right. And Ray . . ."

"Yah."

"I wouldn't spend too much time with Irv, for your own good. His reputation, you know . . . you know what I mean."

"You mean his boozing?"

Dad straightens up and marches back into the store.

"That's exactly what I mean. Now you get on home and tell your mother I'll be along directly."

I grab my jacket and take off while Dad and Agnes finish at the register. Really cold now, and as good as dark. Streetlights are on outside the alley. I'm still shaking, and not from the cold. I don't know why Savre's got it in for me, but . . . well, he's mean. Really *mean,* not just horsing around like a lot of the big guys do.

Darn. Forgot the piano book. I do an about-face. I can walk home with Dad. Funny the difference an hour and a half makes. The alley's dark now, slush freezing up. It's tricky, but I aim for the barrel. It's still glowing and the smoke looks white. Irv's sitting at the little table in the café with Mr. Schweitzer, arguing and laughing and waving his arms. They both are. Jeez, the old cheek hurts.

I hit the bottom step okay but miss the second and bark my shin. "Damn!" And I stop. Don't breathe.

There's a scurrying around inside. The light goes on and swings back and forth. I didn't even notice it was out; he doesn't turn it out till he leaves. Dad says something, I don't know what, and somebody else sounds like she's hurt. Somebody's *crying?* What's going on? What the . . . door's locked. Dad opens it.

"Ray, what's . . . I thought I told you to go home."

He's sweating and pulling on his suit coat, all flustered like he was late for something.

"I forgot my piano music."

Wow! *Bang,* and Agnes comes blasting out of the toilet, pulling on her sweater and coat together. *She's* crying. Really *crying.*

"Ray . . . oh my God. Frank—Mr. Decker—tomorrow, I'll see you tomorrow." And she runs way out the front door. It locks behind her.

Dad sits on the old couch and looks at the floor. He doesn't say a word. He looks old. Well, he *is* old. He's forty-two, but he looks older.

"I forgot my piano book, is all. I put it on the couch."

He picks it up from the floor and hands it to me. No words. Nothing. God, it's creepy.

"So I'll be going. Dad, you coming?"

He sort of grins at me, but it doesn't last and he shakes his head no and waves me out the door. He watches through the little window as I start walking back down the alley. Then I trot a little and then I run and I run and I run down the streets and across the frozen yards, fast as I can go. Down on one knee, up again, run, run. I'm yelling, "No, no, no, *no!*"

Out of breath. Can't get my wind. Jeez, jeez. Damn the piano book. Fling it against the storm door.

Outside light goes on. The door opens.

"Ray?" Mom says. "Supper's ready. What happened to your face?"

# 6

Dad was quiet around the house for a few weeks, for *him,* and Agnes didn't even look at me at the store. I was pretty uncomfortable around the both of them, I have to admit. But now, now that school's almost out for the summer and it's a Saturday noon, Dad's back in form.

"Well, what's on the docket for today, Raymond?"

"Nothing much. I may come down to the store later, or fix the brake on my bike."

"Well, which is it?"

"I don't know yet. Benson might come . . ."

"Yech!" Bud finishes his milk and makes a face. He shakes his head and wipes the back of his hand across his mouth like a movie cowboy who tosses down a shot of rotgut.

"We're going to hike out to Sieferts' pond," he says. "And we won't leave any trail at all because we follow each other's steps *exactly* and the last guy brushes over them with a willow branch so nobody can tell unless they've got the dogs on our trail. But they won't because we'll shake them off when we wade in the creek so they can't pick up our scent and I'm going to—"

"Bud."

"I'm going to discover some swell arrowheads and we'll see some *strange footprints* from somebody who's already *been* there. Only the footprints only go one way, see, so they're still in there, hiding in the cave—"

"Bud, you nut, there isn't any cave by the pond. Besides, it's just an old slough."

He stops and looks up from his plate. He stares at me with his head cocked to one side and looks pretty pleased with himself.

"You just haven't *found* one, Ray. You can't say there ain't one there just because you haven't found one. You ain't that smart, Ray. Maybe I'll go with Maloney and Swenson anyway."

Those are his best buddies, especially Maloney, who also hates girls.

*"Aren't,"* Mom says, and starts gathering up the dinner dishes. "You boys go outside so your father can rest for a while."

My father will try to get a little shut-eye. Every noon and especially on Saturday he stretches out on the davenport in the living room for half an hour until Mom calls him and he goes back to the store. As I say, Agnes does most of the work down there, so he really doesn't need a snooze. I cleaned the store yesterday and did the stock as usual.

"Well, me for a little shut-eye," Dad says.

He stands up and snaps his suspenders and rubs his fists in his eyes like he really needs it and heads for the davenport.

Bud stands up and puts his thumbs in his overall bib and says "Me too," and . . . Well, he can act exactly like Dad when he wants to. He's really good at impersonations, but some people don't appreciate it. Mainly Dad.

Dad whirls around just as Bud is rubbing his eyes exactly the same way.

"Listen, mister," he says. "I've had a long morning and I don't need any smart-aleck—"

"We're going outside. Come on, Bud."

I grab him by the shoulders and scoot him through the back door and we sit on the steps in the sun. We didn't even *talk* about a hike. Maybe he did with Maloney, I don't know. Anyway, three more days and school's out and we'll have the whole summer for hiking if I don't work. And the slough's pretty well dried up. Creek, too.

Wow, it's a peach of a day though. Benson might go. He was over this morning and we fooled around with the model plane we're working on. A Spad with a twenty-four-inch wingspan, all set for the tissue paper. That's the tricky part and he's better at it than I am—getting the tissue paper on the balsa-wood frame and spraying it with water, so it stretches tight when it dries, and putting the lacquer on. Tricky.

"You going to the store, Ray?" Bud talks to his feet.

"No, why?"

"Fix your brake?"

"No I'm not going to fix my brake! *Why?*"

"Well, you told Dad—"

"Oh yah. Well, never mind about that, Bud."

He remembers these silly things. I mean what I told Dad. I do it without even thinking, I guess. Dad's always coming up with "What's on the docket, Ray?" whatever a docket is, or, "What are your plans, Raymond?" And I guess he wants me to say something like "Well, sir, I plan to remodel the living room and paint the garage and plow the back forty and then really get busy," I don't know. So I *do* say some things like planning to go down to the store or fix my brake. It's easier.

When Dad asks Bud what *he* plans to do, Bud says "Nothing." He *used* to ask Bud; now he only asks me. He's got the idea I should plan everything, organize my time, get ahead in the world. Well, to tell the truth, I'm not too interested.

"Boys, your father's gone down to the store," Mom says through the screen door.

She has the dishes washed and she'll take a few minutes to sit down and read a magazine and clip coupons or go next door and chat or just relax and darn some socks. She's not to be bothered though.

"Hey."

Bud jabs my ribs with his elbow.

"Hey, Ray, let's see the plane again. Come on, let's look at the plane."

I push him back on the shoulder and he rolls on the ground and comes back up to a Sitting Bull position.

"Roawww." He puts both hands together like an airplane wing. "Man with wings and twirly nose dives over wigwam, heap big noise, heap big crash—"

"Bud, you watched us all morning. You want to see it again?"

"Sure."

"Oh, all right, come on."

I don't mind, myself. We walk into the house and he steps right in behind me like a shadow, so close that if I stop fast he bangs into me. He does that a lot. Mom's sitting by the front window, clipping a recipe from a magazine. Or a coupon. She sees Bud shadowing me and smiles this time.

We hit the door together, the door to the attic, and bounce back and forth like a couple of drunks. Then I stand back and bow and sweep my arm up the narrow stairs like "after you," and when Bud starts I jump past him and take the stairs in four steps. He comes puffing up, mad as a wet hen. We do this every time.

It's getting hot in our room. I kick my tennis shoes off and the gray painted floorboards feel cool on my bare feet. Bud sees me and does the same. I

66

untie the plane; Benson and I hang it from the ceiling so it won't get smashed before we finish it. And it really does look swell. I like it *before* the paper goes on, like a skeleton with all the wing ribs and fuselage struts and everything.

"Let's have a look, Ray, come on."

Bud brushes a couple of worn-out baseball gloves and an apple core off his bed and sits carefully.

"Okay, but for gosh sakes take it easy."

He balances it in both hands and slowly moves his hands up and down like it's a basket of chicken feathers.

"This is really swell, Ray. It'll fly, too, won't it?"

"Probably. Yah, it should."

I feel good right now. Bud doesn't say stuff like that very often but I can tell he thinks this Spad is pretty special and he isn't old enough to make one. He tries, but he gets too mad. It's nice up in the room with your bare feet on the floor and the sun coming in and your kid brother not horsing around too much. I don't mind the horsing around. It's great, as a matter of fact. Just not all the *time.* Wonder what Gladys is doing? She was going to be busy today, she told me. Helping her mother probably.

I lean back on my bunk bed and run my finger along a crack where the boards come together where the ceiling slants down like the roof. And I whistle "Tiptoe Through the Tulips" between my teeth, not with my lips. I'm practicing that. The whistling, I mean.

"Ray, how many turns is okay?"

Bud's winding the prop and the long rubber band crinkles up. He holds the plane and lets go of the prop. It flutters a few turns and stops. He only wound it a little.

"Probably thirty or forty. Maybe more, we'll have to see what she can take. Benson knows more about that than— *Bud,* don't hold it by the tail when you wind— Bud!"

God, the whole tail assembly cracks off in his hand. The rubber band sags. He drops the busted plane on his bed. He stares at me. Eyes big and black but he's white as a ghost and starting to cry.

I hold my finger right where it was on the ceiling crack. Impossible. Damn, damn, damn. Couldn't have . . . he didn't . . . Jeezus.

"Bud, you *promised.* You *promised,* ya *moron!*"

I lunge for the plane. Bud rolls off the bed, scrambles, hits the landing. Trips. Down the steep steps. A scream and a sound like muskmelons dumped on the floor. Good God Almighty.

I toss the plane and the tail back on his bed and the room spins. No, no, no. Take the steps two at a time and I catch myself just before I land on him. He's dead.

"Bud!"

Mom runs in from the living room. We collide over Bud. She takes a quick breath, puts her hand to her neck. "Oh Lord!"

He's moving. Crumpled up. We kneel over him and straighten him out. His eyes blink, but he's white—God, he's white. Mom tears into the bathroom, wets a washcloth, mops his face and forehead. A bump, a real goose egg on his forehead.

I check his pulse. It's going like crazy but mine is, too, and I don't have a watch anyway. No blood on him, no cuts. Mom feels him all over, starting with his head, all the time saying, "Bud, listen now, it's going to be all right, it's going to be all right."

She stops when she gets to his right leg. It's still bent under him a little and I straighten it while she lifts him up just enough.

"Slowly, Ray, slowly," she says.

He flinches and sucks air like you do when something hurts like sin but you don't want to yell, like Savre's ring on my cheek. But his eyes are open and he looks at me, finally. He's scared. I feel faint. Honest! And *he's* the one who's hurt.

Mom stands and pulls me up. She's breathing hard but she knows what to do.

"You all right, Ray?"

"Sure." *Me* all right!

"Then call Doc Everson's office and tell them we're bringing Bud down. His leg might be broken. And tell your father."

Okay, she gets back to Bud and I skip to the telephone. I lift the receiver and hunch over close to the mouthpiece. Central answers. I tell her about the accident. She says Doc Everson's in his office, thank

God. She'll tell him and she'll call Dad. I have this crazy thought while I hang up the receiver. I think of the tail section of the plane broken off and I think of Bud's bones breaking like that and I think of wrapping tissue paper around his leg and spraying it. He may limp for the rest of his life.

"Ray?"

"All set. No cars that I can see. Westlunds' has a flat. I'll carry him."

"Not five blocks, you won't. Don't be foolish. Just settle down."

"Okay, I'll get the wagon then."

"All right, that'll have to do. Put a quilt in it."

I tear out back, get the old wagon, flip it to get the dirt and leaves out, pull it around front so fast it's up in the air on the turn. Mom and I carry Bud with his arms around us limp and his leg dangling because Mom wrapped a blanket around it. He doesn't fit in the wagon, but most of him does.

I put his leg on a pillow and sort of hold his head and Mom pulls the wagon, whoosh. I've got to scramble to keep up. Bud groans and sucks air whenever the wagon bounces his leg, like whistling through his teeth backwards. But he's okay. He's really okay, I'm sure.

Gladys runs out when we pass her house. "What's wrong, Mrs. Decker? What's the matter with Bud?"

"He's okay, Glad!" I yell. "Can't stop now. Tell you later."

Two blocks down we hit the first curb and Mom's

really puffing. She doesn't talk except in a quiet way to Bud. She turns back and sort of smiles at me. Strange.

Anderson is out by his front steps. Mr. Anderson. He hasn't gone back to the feed mill yet.

"Doc Everson?" he says.

"Yes, thanks," Mom says.

And he just takes the wagon handle and we keep walking fast.

"Ray," Mr. Anderson says, "you take the wagon in case you need it to get him home."

He picks Bud up and just walks downtown with him. He's a tall man, Mr. Anderson, and he hefts those sacks of grain all day. He doesn't say anything. He doesn't ask anything. He just marches right up the squeaky stairs to Doc's office over the dry-goods store. Jeez, it's nice to have him with us. Steps could use an oiling.

"Here, Doc, you got business," he says, and he puts Bud down easy on the table. "Yah, well, good luck. I got to get to work now."

"Thanks, Andy," Doc says. "Well, let's see what we have here. Mrs. Decker, you better sit down while I have a look. Edith." He calls to his girl to look after Mom, but she waves her off.

"No, no," she says. "Doctor, he went down the full flight of stairs—"

"Fourteen steps," I say.

"He seems to be all in one piece, thank God. Hit his head a good one. But the right leg, be sure you check the right leg."

My gosh, she's telling *him* what to do. He nods. I stay by the table, too. The smell of iodine and chloroform and stuff is pretty strong. I was only here once before, when I got a nail through my foot. But Bud looks better.

He peeks around Doc. All I can see is Doc's back, but he's got his stethoscope going and he listens. Then he looks into Bud's eyes, holding the eyelids up. Then he pushes a little on his stomach and moves his arms and legs ever so gently, and tickles Bud's feet. I didn't know Doc could be that gentle.

He doesn't rush. Then he keeps his hand on Bud's leg and tells Mom, "A little crack in the leg. Wouldn't worry about the bump on the head, not with that big a swelling, except he'll have a dandy headache tonight. But I'll swear—stack thirty years of practice on it—that the leg's just a hairline fracture; doesn't even need setting. Course I can X-ray it if you want, but I'd have to charge, oh—"

"No, you go ahead and forget the X ray. I'm not all that keen on X rays anyway."

So Doc tells Bud, "We'll give you a little something to show your friends. And you stay off that leg for—oh, four weeks. Give it a little time to knit and you'll be as good as new."

He's not so gentle when he slaps the cast on. Up to his elbows in gauze and hot plaster and stuff. He's good. I mean he knows how to do it. You can tell when somebody really knows what he's doing.

Like Irv knows *his* job. Bud screws up his face a few times but doesn't say anything. He hasn't said anything since it happened.

So we're through. Just like that. I'm a little woozy and Mom looks red-faced and tired. It's really hot. Stuffy. And in walks Pete, who works for Anderson down at the mill.

"I got the truck outside," he says.

So Doc himself carries Bud down and puts him in the Ford in back. I sit back there with him and the quilt and the pillow and the wagon. Mom sits up with Pete and folds the blanket on her lap and home we go.

We put him on the davenport with the cast up on some pillows to keep the leg from swelling up the first couple of days, Doc said. Mom goes out in the kitchen and calls back, "Pete, how about a glass of lemonade?" but he's already on his way back to the mill. "Well, we'll have some," she says.

"You still mad, Ray?"

Bud looks up at the ceiling, but at least he's talking.

"Mad? No, why should I be?"

"But you *were*. About the plane. I didn't mean it, I swear."

There's a couple of tears running down his cheek now. That really gets me. Here it is, sunny and school almost out, and I'm feeling like it's the saddest day of winter.

"Aw, forget the plane. We'll do another one.

Benson won't care either, you'll see."

I go help Mom squeeze the lemons. Trouble is, I *was* mad. But I wasn't going to knock him down the stairs. Maybe he thought I was, I don't know. Smash the lemon half down and twist it around. The smell makes spit come to my mouth. I wouldn't have knocked him down the stairs.

Dad. I clean forgot about Dad until right this minute when the front door slams. Where's he *been?*

This time it doesn't take long to find out. Had to wait for Agnes to get back, went to Doc's but we'd left, walked home, what's this all about and where's Ray. That's before he even gets to the davenport.

"Bud, Doc tells me you're fine, but what *happened?*"

Bud doesn't say anything. In the first place he's in no shape for a lot of talk anyway. I squeeze the old lemons, drop them into the pitcher, chip a little ice off the block in the icebox.

"We're in the kitchen, Frank," Mom says. "Bud needs to rest."

She pours tall glasses of lemonade, four of them, and gives me two. I bump into Dad going around the corner.

"Ray," he says.

Just "Ray." Terrific. He recognizes me. I give one of the glasses to Bud and keep the other and sit on the throw rug by the davenport.

"Ice in it!"

"Yah, a little. Good, huh, Bud?"

My father sits down in his chair in the dining room. I don't have to see it to know it. He sighs and sucks air through his teeth. False teeth, some of them. He leaves them in a glass in the bathroom at night.

"Raymond!" he shouts. "I'd like to know, if it's not too much trouble . . . I'd like to know just what's going on here."

"Yah, Dad."

I shrug my shoulders at Bud, leave my glass on the rug, and go into the dining room.

"Frank, Bud had an accident—"

"I *know* that, Laura. Central told me that and Doc told me that and I can see that. What I want to know is—"

"And he's going to be fine, thank God."

Mom stands by the table and brushes some hair back from her forehead.

"Well, of course that's good, of course."

My father sips his lemonade and mops his face with his folded-up handkerchief.

"But tell me, Ray. Tell me just how you could let a thing like this happen, will you tell me that?"

I don't believe it. Yes I do. All of a sudden I feel so darn tired, like after a long winter hike when you can't hardly lift your foot up to get the overshoe off. Then I say this crazy thing.

"Dad, look, what happened was I threw him down the steps just for the hell of it, but that didn't work so I broke his leg with the baseball bat!"

"Hah!" Bud snorts from the other room.

It's just that I'm so pooped out. My father sits there clicking his teeth. Looks like a beet. Really going to pop. He slams his hands down on the table and jumps up and knocks the chair over and I don't really know what's going to happen. Don't really care.

Then he looks at me. That's better.

"I don't need that from anyone, you understand?"

His voice is trembly, sort of a whine like a buzz saw in cordwood.

"You've got responsibilities, you know those responsibilities, and this is no time to be a smart aleck!"

Mom says, "Frank, Ray wasn't—"

"He can answer for himself, Laura. Raymond can answer for himself."

"I know he can," she says. "You just give him the chance."

So he looks at me again, and I suppose better now than later.

"Okay. Bud and I went up to look at the plane after you went to the store and it broke partly and Bud tripped on the landing and fell down the stairs. And then Mom and I and Mr. Anderson—"

"Bud broke the plane? His plane?"

"The Spad. I told you; the one Benson and I are making. It's not the end of the world or anything."

"And you had a fight or what? How could he

just fall down the stairs if you were taking care of him?"

Dad's looking out the window. He keeps an eye on me in the reflection.

"I stumbled," Bud says from the davenport. "Everybody stumbles. *You* even stumble. Not Ray's fault."

"Dad, I went over to see about the plane and maybe Bud thought I was mad at him. Well, I *was* right then. But he tripped on the landing and—"

"All right. Allll right. That's enough."

He waves his arms like an umpire signaling safe.

"I thought so, Ray. I didn't want to, but I suspected you could have prevented—"

"Frank," Mom says, "we've been through enough for one day. I mean enough!"

She stands up with her hands on her hips and looks him right in the face. He starts out, "I just want to—"

"No, Frank, that's *enough.*" And she stares him down! Can you beat that?

He sticks his handkerchief back in his pocket. Jeez, I'm beat. Then he walks around the table and through the living room.

"I'll talk to you tomorrow, Raymond. Don't bother coming to the store."

And he's out the door. Slam again.

Mom and I sit there. It's quiet all through the house. She pats me on the arm.

"Mom, why in the hell does he—"

"Ray!"

"Sorry. Well, why this again? Why make such a problem? He always does."

"Most of the time, that's true."

"And it seems that I'm always the . . . what's the word?"

"Victim?"

"I guess. I mean he just blames me for every darn . . . I bet he blames me when he's constipated, that'll be next."

Mom brushes some hair from her face and fans her cheek with a napkin.

"As I've told you, Ray." She lowers her voice so Bud can't hear. He can hear mice breathing when he wants to. "As I've told you, your father has faults, and—"

"Yah, but so does everybody, don't they?"

"He is a drinking man."

"I *know* that, but not as bad as a lot."

"And he's a man who needs more than one woman, if you follow me. I gave up on that years ago, right after Bud was born, and—"

"Mom, why don't *you* tell him to lay off us kids, huh? You can do it, I know. I mean these big scenes with Bud and me over every little . . . well, just tell him to lay *off!*"

She stands and picks up her glass. And she smiles. I haven't said anything funny that I know of.

"Oh, I will, Ray, I will when the time is right.

But you're the one who'll really bring him to his knees, Ray. *You.* I just know it."

"I don't want to bring—"

"And it's coming, sure as God made little green apples. Now don't worry yourself, Ray."

Smiling again. And she marches into the kitchen.

Don't worry myself. Hah! Well, anyway, I see Bud's finished his lemonade. Mine's warm but I gulp it down without stopping and feel like throwing the glass as hard as I can.

"Ray, I'm sorry."

"Just forget it, Bud. Forget it."

"No, I mean about Dad."

I run up to our room and take the old Spad in both hands, both pieces. I crunch it into match-sticks and step on it hard with my bare feet. Just balsa wood. Jeez, sometimes it's hard to keep from, you know . . . crying.

# 7

I'm plunking out "Red Sails in the Sunset" on the piano, waiting for Mom and Dad to come home from church. He went this morning for the first time since Easter and I stayed with Bud.

Bud had a rough time last night and Mom was up two or three times to give him some aspirin, but he's okay. Really. This morning he was aiming an invisible bow and arrow at his big toe sticking out of the cast and going, "Twannng, ahhh!" Killing his toe, for crying out loud. He's okay.

It all happened just yesterday but it seems like a year ago. Mrs. Westlund and some other neighbors dropped by to see if they could help and Mrs. Fenster brought over a salmon hot dish, which wasn't bad, and Dad didn't get back from the store until I was asleep. There they are.

Mom asks Bud how he's feeling and he says, "Fine." Dad just sits with the Sunday paper. No talk. Well, no talk from me either.

In fact, no talk through Sunday dinner. Chicken and mashed potatoes and gravy and string beans and rice pudding and I don't even taste it. Bud has his on a tray in the spare room, the study. That's where he'll sleep now. Me too, to keep an eye on him. I don't mind that.

So now Mom's washing the dishes and Dad's fiddling with the paper again and I'm wondering what Gladys is up to and Reverend Parker comes to the front door.

That's right! The *minister* comes right up to our door and knocks, and says he's there to see *me*. In he comes. I *wondered* why Dad left his suit coat on, and why he went to church in the first place.

"Good of you to come, good of you to come," Dad says.

Reverend Parker says, "No trouble, no trouble at all. Glad to be of help, Frank. Glad to be of help."

I get edgy when grownups keep saying everything twice.

Parker sits down in the big chair with his hat on his lap. He looks at me over his glasses. I'm sitting on the piano bench and Dad's on the davenport looking at Parker. Reverend Parker. What little surprises do we—

"Well," Reverend Parker says.

No more. Just "Well." He looks better with his robe on. Then he gets into his visit. The crux of the matter, as Irv says.

"And your brother, Raymond, how is your brother?"

"Fine, Reverend Parker. He's in the spare room. You want to—"

"And what are we to do about this, eh? Just what are we to do?"

"About Bud?"

"Raymond," Dad says, *"listen* to the Reverend."

I'm listening. Boy, am I listening. I just don't hear anything, is all.

"Frank, it's all right," Parker says. He smiles just like at the potluck or when he tells a joke during the sermon, so you know it's a joke and it's okay to snicker or blow your nose or cough. It drives me crazy.

"I'm afraid, Raymond, that it's more than just Bud," he says. "From what your father tells me, it's more than that, yes."

He looks at his hat and takes off his glasses and pinches his nose where they leave a crease. Mom has stopped washing dishes, I can tell.

"I'm afraid that we have a problem here. A problem, shall we say, of responsibility, respect, Christian love."

"We do?"

I can feel the old mashed potatoes trying to come up. We should open a window or something.

"Yes, we do."

He looks at Dad and shakes his head ever so slightly. And here I am, jittery and sick to my stomach with the minister and all, and *still* I'm getting sleepy. What about *that.* Reverend Parker does that to me. He could make me feel sleepy in a burning barn.

"All right, Raymond," he says. "I must say I was surprised when your father came to me with—"

"Me too."

"Ray!" Dad yells.

"With this problem. I agree that, given the chance, you can learn from this, Raymond. Learn and become a better person for it, a better Christian and servant of God. You'll stay with your brother during his confinement, and you will not neglect him or make things more difficult for your father. And mother. And you will meditate on these things each day, Raymond. On brotherly love, on the God-given responsibilities of Christian brotherhood, on honoring your father and mother, and . . . and the sins of provocation. Do you understand what I'm saying?"

"Well . . ."

"Would you like a cup of coffee, Mr. Parker?" my mother asks in a loud voice. She stands in the archway to the dining room with her apron still on over her nice blue dress. "I have some still hot from dinner." She smiles at Parker and keeps smiling.

"No, no, thank you, Laura. Not . . . well, no, thank you anyway."

She just stands there. Parker waits for her to leave but she doesn't, so he swings back to me.

"All right, I believe you can understand the need for this, Raymond, the cleansing it can bring you."

"Oh, sure." I mean I've got to say *something*.

"It's just that I don't understand the details, I guess. I mean thinking about these things, sure, but I'd be helping Bud anyway and—"

"Raymond," he says, putting his glasses back on. "Raymond, your father feels this strongly and I must say I agree. It can be a turning point for you. You will stay with your brother during his confinement, that is for one month starting after school is out on Tuesday."

Now we're getting to the crux.

"You will tend to his needs. You will not venture outside without your father's permission. And you will meditate on these things. Also . . ."

He shoots a look at my father, who says, "Obedience."

"Yes. You will promise, you will give me your word in Christ that you will be obedient to your father. And mother. Do you understand that?"

"Well, yes, sure, but I don't know why I—"

"Fine, Raymond. Now if we may have a moment of prayer for the redemption of this soul."

He wants it over with. Me too. Mom stomps back into the kitchen, slams the coffeepot on the range, runs water in the sink.

"Father, we ask thy mercy on this young man, one of your . . ."

My father's bowing his head. His damn bald head. His idea, the whole crazy—

". . . to be indeed our brother's keeper and accept our responsibilities with a cheerful . . ."

Damn his bald head. Jeez, I gave my word. Not really, but just as good as—

". . . that he may come to increased awareness of the bountiful blessings which thou hast bestowed upon . . ."

Parker should *preach,* not go around messing in people's affairs. . . .

". . . and to learn from our mistakes. Lord, we are all sinners. In Jesus' name. Amen."

And he's out the door in nothing flat. My father shuts the door and loosens his tie and asks me if it's all clear to me. I nod. Not queasy anymore. He grins like he's doing me a favor. No talking with him, no sir. None. If we're all sinners, okay, and that includes *him.*

Mom stands in the archway again and says in a very quiet voice that sounds sort of like a far-off yell, "The next time—*any*time—you have something like this in mind for either of our children, Frank Decker, you let me know. You talk it over with me first, just like store decisions. Do *you* understand?"

He just nods his head. It's strange.

# 8

Well, Benson knows about it because I told him yesterday. And Miss Golie knows about it because I had to tell her. She's Bud's teacher and he's missing the last two days of school. And I told Gladys.

Oh, hell, *everybody* knows about it, everybody in the county probably. It was up to me to tell Miss Golie, my father said Sunday night, and I just nodded. No talk, no sir. He was so happy he went to bed singing the Barbasol song they sing on the radio for this *shaving* cream. Forty degrees off key, it doesn't matter.

Today's the last day of school. It's a great day usually. Some of the guys are skipping school and horsing around. You don't do much and finals are over and you get out early and you turn in books and say good-bye to teachers, especially those who won't be back. And they ask what you're going to do over the summer and you say not much and they say well stay out of trouble.

Everybody's watching me, they really are. Benson says they aren't, but I know better. So does he.

This is my last class, Miss Martin's history. She's

leaving. Won't be back next year, and I wouldn't have her anyway. I'm the last one. Most all the rest are outside. Usually I'm not last but I have this headache. Hungry, maybe.

Miss Martin looks up and lets her glasses hang by the black velvet ribbon. She's surrounded by books on her desk, but she balances mine on top.

"There, that does it," she says. "Ray, I'm going to miss you."

Jeez, I'm glad the rest of the kids left. Plunkett stops by the door and then runs down the hall. Another buddy of mine, sort of.

"Well, I hope you have a nice summer, Miss Martin."

She stands and walks around her desk and puts her arm on my shoulders—*her arm on my shoulders*—and walks me to the classroom door.

"I was sorry to hear about your brother."

"Oh, he'll be okay."

"I'm sure he will. Ray, I'll say good-bye now. Keep up your reading, will you? Not just for school, for *you*."

Then I don't believe it. She shakes my hand and leans over and gives me a quick kiss on the forehead. Jeez. I mean she's nice and all, but I don't know.

" 'Bye, Miss Martin."

I almost run down the hall, past some kids cleaning out their lockers, and out the front door. They're standing around in bunches. There's Plunkett with some of the guys. I *knew* it. He heard.

"I'm going to *miss* you, Raymond, dear!" he shouts, and they all laugh. "Hey, Decker, how's the old leg breaker?"

Some of the girls laugh, too. One over near Gladys I don't see says, "Raymond, dear, whatcha got planned for the summer? Something real exciting?"

Oh, the hell with it. What difference does it make? The guys catch up with me and sort of trail along across the courthouse square. Benson's with me.

"Come on, you guys, leave him be," he says. "Go play with your marbles or something. Go play with your old whanger."

"Hey, Deck."

It's Plunkett again, right beside me. He's not a bad guy but I wish he'd shut up. Right now I wish he'd shut up. I got to get home.

"Yah, Plunkett."

"*My* brother broke his arm last year."

"I know."

"But I didn't push him down the stairs or anything. Jeez, Deck, can't you pick on—"

"I didn't either, Plunkett."

"No, he didn't," Gladys says from somewhere, and her friends giggle. I wish she'd keep out of this.

"No, leave me alone, Plunkett, I'm not kidding."

I stop and look right at him when I say this but my voice is shaky. Sounds shaky.

"And I sure as hell didn't have to stay in the

house for a whole *month.*" He's talking back to the rest of them, not to me. "A whole *month.* Decker's got to play nursemaid for a whole—"

I shove Benson aside and bash Plunkett in the belly. Hard. He's a friend, but . . . ooofta, right in the belly and he goes down with no air. I'm on him. I'm kind of crying and yelling "Damn, damn, damn you," and punching him on the back and I could break him in half. I could. I roll him over and sit on him. Spread his arms out in the gravel. Look right down in his face. He's scared. He gets one arm loose and cracks me on the nose. Yelling. Blam. Everybody's yelling. I crack him and grab the arm and twist.

"Give up? Want some more, Plunkett, you bastard?"

Pulling up. Somebody's pulling me up under the arms. Benson. I toss him off but he grabs me again.

"Come on, Deck. He's had enough."

I guess he has. He's crying now, rubbing his face, nose running. Muddy, bloody tears. He's a friend, but damn him. The guys start walking away.

"Didn't have to jump me, Deck. Just horsing around. Jeez, I know your old man."

Still sniffling. Benson walks partway home with me. I'm shaking like a leaf again. Like it was twenty below. Bleeding a little from the nose. Knuckles skinned. Sick to my stomach now. Dizzy.

"You all right?"

Benson brushes himself off and Gladys catches

up. We walk along.

"Hell yes, I guess so. Why not?" Sucking air through my mouth and deep down. Really winded.

"Ray, you were very brave."

Oh good Lord. *Brave.* Gladys is trying to be nice, I guess, but . . . most girls seem to like fights, really *like* them. Maybe because they're not in them, I don't know.

"Okay, Gladys," Benson says. He's not too keen on her. "Deck, you really waded into him, and your face is messed up. Pants, too. Look, I got to get home, but don't worry. I mean Plunkett won't snitch. Neither will Gladys, will you, Glad?"

"Snitch? Of course not."

So we split up and I'm in the bathroom. Dad's not home for dinner yet. I brush the mud off my knickers and wash the blood off my knuckles and face. No damage. I keep pulling up handfuls of water and splash them against my face even after it's clean. Feels good.

I'll be okay. Plunkett won't blab. Probably washing up at his house, same as I am here. Some guys would, but he won't. And I'm going to look fine for dinner. Here comes my father from the store. Everything went fine at school today and he's not going to get one more word out of me, that's for sure.

# 9

Three weeks down and a week to go. It's still cool because it's still early. The morning breeze is good, but I can smell the heat on the way, sort of like baked cornstalks.

It'll be hot and dry again, the worst summer in God knows how long. Another year of practically no crops and that's tough on everybody, not just the farmers. Some runty corn, hardly enough hay for feed, a little wheat, practically no oats and barley. More farms up for sale. And some days after weeks of no rain, the wind is black, just blowing the top-soil away. Gets in your eyes and in through windows. I guess it was worse a few years back, that's what they say.

Even the river's dry. The bottom has cracks in it big enough to throw a cat in, if you're in the habit of throwing cats around. I've been reading a lot of Mark Twain and he says a lot about cats. Dead, mainly. We get drinking water from Fensters' well. I saw the river a few days ago and Mom knew it. Stuff all over the bottom. Old tires, barrel hoops, rolls of snow fence, an iron range that some guys dragged out on the ice last winter.

I've been awake since four-thirty, just for the heck of it. I can wake up when I want to about nine times out of ten. It's crazy waking up at that hour, because the best time to sleep this June is between two in the morning and about eight. I've tested it. I've had plenty of time.

Bud and I still sleep here in the study. But we do when the weather gets hot anyway, broken leg or no broken leg. Dad still calls this his study and he's got a set of encyclopedias in here that he says he refers to but he doesn't. Bud and I put them all upside down last fall and he didn't even notice. They're pretty good, too.

I do keep thinking about my father, I can't help it. Why should I care if he calls the spare room a study, if it makes him happy? But I do. The whole thing's so phony. And he does hit the bottle like Mom says, but not bad. He doesn't go down in the basement and drink and then hang himself like Benson's dad did. And Benson was the one who found him, too. And he doesn't skip town like so many guys, although there's plenty of times I wish he *would*.

He's splashing water in the bathroom now, just hands and face, and shaving and cutting himself and sticking little pieces of wet toilet paper on the cuts. He takes them off when they dry, usually at the breakfast table, and they bleed a little more. I could get along without him bleeding when I'm eating my Rice Krispies.

Bud's stirring in the other cot. Oh, yah, these are regular army cots, not bed cots. The reason is we've got the regular bunk beds up in our attic room, but when we set them up last year, Dad wanted extra screws in just to be on the safe side.

"But they're solid as a church, Dad," I told him.

"No, no, better be safe than sorry, Raymond. We'll just put the extra screws in."

"But I don't—"

"Now no fussing. A stitch in time saves nine, as they say. Let this be a lesson to you."

Well, it was. In the first place, I did all the screwing until my arm was about to drop off, and now we can't get the beds apart without dynamite. They're going to be there till the house comes down.

That's why Bud and I have the army cots down here. Actually, they're a heck of a lot cooler than the beds but if I said that, he'd say that's what he had in mind, and he hasn't even thought of it.

Bud bangs his cast against the wall and jerks up awake, falls back on the pillow and sits up again. This time he braces himself with his arms back. A pillow just makes it hotter, but he claims he gets a charley horse in his arm if he doesn't sleep with a pillow. A charley horse in his *arm,* the loon.

"What's going on, Ray?"

"What you mean, what's going on?"

"I mean what time is it? Are you awake?"

"Of course I'm awake. I'm talking, aren't I? I'm

sitting on the cot with my eyes open, aren't I? *Are you awake!*"

Bud swings the leg with the cast over the edge of his cot and onto a kitchen stool that's just the right height. He can do it without even thinking now and without tipping the cot over, the way he first did.

The cot used to go over and Dad would yell, "Ray, don't let him do that!" So Mom and I borrowed a short kitchen stool from Mrs. Westlund and Bud got used to that. We went right over to Westlunds'. And Bud and I have been out for a while nearly every day, at least in the backyard. And Benson and the guys have been over and I've gone for walks like when I saw the river. It's not like we're in solitary confinement. Mom knows about all this and Dad's so darn happy about the arrangement he conned Reverend Parker into—or Reverend Parker conned *me* into—that he doesn't bother checking.

So now Bud sits there with just his underwear shorts on and looks at the cast. It goes from right under his knee to his toes. He's looked at it a million times, but he won't let anybody write on it. Well, he did let me, but around in back where nobody would see. And he let Maloney, but Maloney wrote big and he got mad.

"I got to go to the toilet," he says.

"Me too."

"No, I really do. I really have to *go.*"

So I stand by the bathroom door and Bud starts

climbing off the cot with his crutch. He likes the old crutch by now. Calls it Morgan, don't ask me why. "Morgan and I are going into the living room," he'll say.

I talk to my father only on business, but this is business.

"Dad. Daaad. Bud needs to get into the bathroom."

The faucets jam off hard and vibrate the pipes in the basement. He says something I can't hear clearly and then comes out smelling like shaving cream and he has water drops on his hands and face. And pieces of toilet paper. He holds a hand towel and he's got his pants and socks and shoes on. He always puts his pants and socks and shoes on before he shaves.

"Yes?"

"Dad, Bud needs to use the—"

"I *know*. I heard you the first time. So just stand aside and let him use it."

I'm not in the way, but I'm not arguing either.

"Raymond, stand *aside.*"

I back up almost to the living room. He still never really looks at me, but I look at him. He looks at the top of my head or around my ears, not at my eyes. Now he goes into their bedroom, wiping his hands on the towel and wiping the back of his neck. He's got hair on his shoulders, too.

Bud's already in the bathroom, pissing away like there was no tomorrow. Urinating we call it because of Mom. And that's all right. At least it's not weewee or number one or something like that, the way it is with Plunkett's kid sister. Hey, Plunkett came over one day outside the window, and I opened the screen and we shook hands. Pretty good.

Mom calls from the kitchen. I pull on my overall pants and help Bud with his, but he wants to do it himself. He's got the right pants leg cut up to the knee—Mom did that—so it slops around but it's easy to get on.

Dad comes out of the bedroom with his shirt and bow tie on. He hums something that's not a tune and pushes by me. He's pulling up his suspenders one at a time. Nothing looks crazier than suspenders hanging down like sagging sheets on a clothesline.

"Just remember, Raymond, why this whole thing had to be done and what you're  . . ."

"What I'm *what?*"

He's already in the kitchen and I can't hear for a sec. Mom calls out in a loud voice, "He said, what you're supposed to be learning out of all this bother." And Dad blasts out the *back* door. Mom smiles and fixes the breakfast tray for Bud.

As if I could forget. The thing is, I don't think anybody really knows. Dad hasn't discussed it, Parker hasn't mentioned it since his big performance that Sunday at our house. Mom hasn't. And *I* sure haven't.

# 10

A couple of days to go and you can't stay inside during summer vacation when it's sunny and the grass is already up and turning brown and the sky is clear as far as you can see. I can't anyway.

So it's wrong. We've done it before. I pull Bud in the wagon and Mom knows, but she just waves from the kitchen window. We cut across backyards.

"Hey, Ray," Bud says when we duck under some lilac bushes.

"Hey what?"

"Hey, this is Westlunds' backyard."

"So?"

"Well, where are we going anyways, you tell me that. That girl could be around."

"Gladys? Bud, call her by name, for gosh sakes, don't sound like such a dope. Yah, she might be at that."

I flip the wagon handle back to Bud, like it is when you push the wagon. He's not too happy and his leg itches inside the cast, I know. But I'll tell you, there are times when he can be a real pest. Mainly with girls. I look around and Gladys isn't out feeding her rabbits, anyway. She's got a hutch of rabbits out by the shed. I thought she might be, is all.

"Let's go."

"Where, Bud? You know the rules. We aren't even supposed to be this far."

"So we go back or what?"

"Naw. Let's just rest for a minute."

I push him into the shade and I stroll on the Westlunds' garden walk. I've done it lots of times. Nothing much is up in the garden except radishes and they're always up. I could go the rest of my life without another radish.

I whistle a tune between my teeth. I'm still working on that, to pass the time. "My Man" is what I'm whistling. Gladys' rabbits are probably dying of thirst. I mean it's *hot.*

There she is. At the kitchen window. Got a blue ribbon in her hair.

"Ray, let's go home," Bud says.

"You just keep quiet and have a good time."

"Hi Ray, Bud. Wait a minute." She disappears from the window.

A second later she bounces out the screen door. I mean she's got a white skirt on with the pleats that make a guy dizzy. And a blue blouse with short puffy sleeves. Gosh, she's all dressed up on a weekday. That's all right with me. Any old time.

"Hi, boys."

Hi *boys!* She swings down the garden walk to

meet me and the pleats go in and out when she twirls around.

"Like it, Ray?"

"Yah. Oh, yah, it's very nice, the skirt, the outfit. Looks really great, Glad. I thought your rabbits needed water."

*Rabbits.* Jeez, when I sound like an idiot, I sound like an *idiot.* She laughs.

"Rabbits? Don't be silly, Ray. Dad got rid of them *weeks* ago."

"Did he drown 'em or shoot 'em or what?" Bud asks.

"I haven't the faintest idea, really. How's your leg?"

"Fine."

"Didn't you come over to see me, Ray, or are you simply mad about my rabbits? Let's go out in front, shall we?"

She laughs again and sort of dances by herself and I could sit there and watch that till the cows come home. Wow. But with a little less laughing. That phony kind anyway.

*"Course* I came over to see you, Glad. I was about to knock."

"Call me 'Westie.' "

"Hah!" Bud snorts.

"No, really, that's what my friends call me now. Sounds like more fun than Gladys, don't you think, Ray? Really?"

And she twirls again and the blouse billows out

and there's the brassiere strap. She really needs it. The brassiere, I mean. Has for months. Jeez, she just reaches up and puts the strap back over her shoulder without even going into the front porch or anything.

"Something wrong?" she says with a smile.

"Wrong? Not at all. No, don't be silly. No."

Jeez, I've got to stop *talking* like that. Bud starts to climb out of the wagon. He can walk all right with the crutch. So I tear home with him in the wagon, hand him his crutch, and tear back. He doesn't complain, because his buddy Maloney is there.

She hasn't moved. She looks surprised to see me, but it's one of those fake surprises like when you tell a girl that's a nice scarf she's wearing and she's suddenly surprised to even see it there. "Oh, this old thing? I forgot I had it on." Forgot, my foot!

"So you decided to come back."

"Sure. Just had to get Bud home. He's all right."

I'm panting and I'm sweating through my old shirt. Through my khakis, too, but it doesn't show as much there. She looks like she *never* sweats, I swear, and we walk into the front yard.

Another twirl, two times around. Jeez.

"Ray, you really like me in this?"

"I told you I did. Yah, Glad—"

" 'Westie.' "

"Yah, Gladys, you look terrific. Honest you do."

She frowns in the sunlight and looks up and

down the street, blond curls swinging.

"I mean it's not too cute or anything?"

"Well, it's cute, sure it's cute. But I wouldn't say too cute, I guess."

I sit down cross-legged under a spindly elm. She won't sit down in that skirt, I know. If she sat down right beside me now, I'd have to move. She watches the corner but keeps talking to me.

"You *guess*. I mean does it make me look younger or older or what? I'm just curious."

"Oh, well, older, no question. Definitely older."

I didn't know what she was fishing for until now. And she really does look older. She used to be skinny but now she's slender and has curves. Funny, but everybody calls girls skinny, if they are, up to about our age and then they call them slender. Same with boys. All my life I've been skinny and now grownups call me lanky.

"You going someplace, Gladys?"

" 'Westie.' Can't you call me 'Westie'?"

"Well, if that's what you want, but it'll take a while to get used to, Glad. Just sounds strange at first."

It sounds awful, as a matter of fact, and I'll be damned if I'm going to.

"You going someplace?"

"A little tennis, Ray. Sound like fun?"

"Tennis!"

I'm looking at the back of her neck where the curls bounce. She does sweat, but just a little.

"You can't play tennis, Glad."

"Well, I can learn. Don't be silly."

"No, I mean the old court's full of weeds and nobody's played there for years. There isn't even a *net*."

There's a car, backfiring like mad. Oh no. Savre's Model A coupe. Nothing can happen here. Wait it out till he's passed. He graduated, God knows how. Off for St. Olaf next fall and they can have him.

I stand up and put my hands in my pockets, sort of lounging against the tree. I have to. I mean with Gladys twirling around that way with those pleats, and the curls bouncing up and down, and the strap coming down. Well, all of a sudden I'd stick out in front if I didn't have my hands in my pockets. Just since I sat under—

"Westie. Hop in!"

Good God Almighty, he pulls up *here* and she skips out to the car. He's got his *letter sweater* on. Ninety in the shade and a white wool letter sweater. I don't believe it. Yes I do.

But she can't—I mean he's—I mean she's just thirteen . . . no, fourteen. Birthday last month. I gave her a card with a pretty syrupy poem on it.

" 'Bye, Ray. Nice chatting with you, really."

She hops in the car and slams the door. I guess her mother isn't home.

Savre leans out the window. Here it comes. He holds out two beat-up old tennis rackets.

"If it isn't Raymond Decker, champeen leg

breaker. How ya doin', kid? Naw, hell, just kidding. Don't get sore and start bawling or something."

I give a snort of disgust, but darn, my nose starts running like mad and I can't get at my handkerchief. Maybe they wouldn't see; yes, they would. I turn my back to them partway, so they can't see, and trip a little on an elm root. Savre's looking at Gladys.

"Westie, you're sure you want to play tennis?" And he laughs. "Sure your boyfriend here won't mind?"

My ears are hot and I feel stupid turned this way like Barney the cripple. I wouldn't mind slitting Savre's throat, letter sweater and all. I've still got a scar from that class ring.

"Oh, Ray and I are just good friends," she says in a loud voice. "Neighbors and friends, isn't that right, Ray? 'Bye now, and say hello to your mother for me."

I really don't believe it. I don't say a word. They're off in a spray of gravel and dust. Tennis, my foot.

Wow. I straighten up and drag out the handkerchief and blow my nose a good one. Don't need the hands in the pockets now. Wouldn't mind slitting Glad's throat too, while I'm at it. Naw. Naw, I take that back. But Jeez, I thought we had things worked out. Not in so many words, but everybody *knows* we've been going steady. Of course I've been out of things. Damn the Rev and Dad. And Bud's busted leg. And guys like Savre. *Damn the whole cockeyed world!*

I tromp back to the house, not just walk. It's good to stomp the ground with each step and in the back door and through the kitchen and . . .

"Ray, Bud's in the study. How's Gladys?"

"Fine, just *fine.*"

"Good. The Maloney boy went home."

"Her name is 'Westie.' "

Mom puts down her darning and I march through the living room.

"What *are* you talking about?"

"That's right, and she's going to be a gorgeous tennis star and she poisoned all her rabbits and she doesn't need guys like me hanging around and I sure as hell *don't need her!*"

Mom doesn't say anything, just rocks and darns more socks. I sneak a look and she's smiling! I slam the door and flop on a cot. No crying or anything, not even close. Just, well, very surprised, you might say. And *mad.* I didn't think I could get mad at Gladys, but boy! Bud's on the other cot staring at the ceiling.

"Ray."

"Yah!"

"Did Savre give you the business?"

"Naw. How did you know he—"

"Heard his flivver. When the cast is off, I'll kick him again if you want. I don't mind, really."

He's serious. I *do* feel a little like tears now, but

that's no good and I swallow fast. I'm sweating like a horse, but it's drying.

"Ray, you stay away from that girl and everything'll be swell."

"It's not that simple."

"But girls are no damn *good,* Ray. They don't even like frogs."

I want to laugh, because what does he know. Advice from a kid brother. But instead I take a deep breath.

"Bud, you're probably right, at that."

Tennis!

# 11

Freedom! The month was over yesterday. I've been keeping track on a little calendar in my billfold and Bud's been marking days on his cast, around in back. Four straight lines and then a fifth line through at an angle, like Robinson Crusoe.

After Dad went to the store this morning, I walked all over town and saw a lot of the guys. Not much doing, but it's good just to move around. Didn't see Gladys, but then I wasn't looking very hard either. Then I got to thinking. Irv asked about Bud when I stopped by the newspaper. "You mean he's still got the cast on?" he said. But he was busy, so I didn't hang around. Now that I'm home for dinner, it's nagging at me.

There's Dad. We go through dinner without much talk, as usual. Nearly everything's between Mom and Dad. "Pass the bread, please." "More green beans, anyone?" "How are things at the store?" "Just dandy." "Beautiful day." "Mmm." "Please." "Thank you." "Excuse me."

But I'm not too keen on this silence anymore. It just doesn't make sense. So when he's ready to go back, I talk to him.

"Dad, I'll take Bud down this afternoon and get that cast off, okay? Doc said just four weeks, and it itches like crazy."

He stops in the doorway.

"Raymond, I think I'm capable of making that decision. Time enough for that next week. You just see that he's comfortable. What's this I hear about you traipsing all over town?"

It's just like he doesn't even know that the time's up! But he knows. He's got to know. That's enough of this business. I follow him to the front door.

"Look, Dad, I'm just trying—"

"Like I said, Raymond, next week and no back-talk. You've learned *that* by now, I hope."

He doesn't even turn around. So.

I horse around with Bud for a few minutes and then I tell him.

"Bud, listen."

"Yah?"

"Come on, we're going to get that cast off."

"We *are?* Ain't you in enough—"

"Aren't. Don't you want it off? Come on, we've put in our time and you've had it on longer than Doc said."

"Yah, sure, but—"

"No buts. Bring your tennis shoes."

"I can walk on it fine, Ray."

"I know, I know. With the cast off you can run. *Mom,* Bud and I are going downtown to see Doc.

Back in plenty of time for supper with the cast off."

Without even coming out of the kitchen, she says, "Fine, Ray. Bud, good luck."

So we start out in the wagon, but we soon drop that. It's squeaky; needs oil. It's silly, too. It's easier for Bud to walk, so we do.

We go right up to Doc's office but he isn't there. It's stuffy again, same old smells, but it doesn't seem so bothersome this time. Then he comes wheeling in and says, "Hey, I was wondering when you'd be around. That thing should come off."

And he cracks it and saws a little and snips with a big scissors, and it pops right off without even hurting. Bud's leg looks funny, like your fingers when you stay in the bathtub too long on a Saturday night, which Bud never does. We can see the scratches, too, where he used the scratcher I made out of a coat hanger.

Bud walks around for Doc and jumps and Doc gives him a pat on the rear and says, "Okay, young man. Good as new. Get out and get some fresh air."

That's it.

When we get home, after Bud goes hopping and skipping all over, Mom takes a careful look at his white leg. Doc offered him the old cast for a keepsake but he didn't want it and I wasn't surprised. Mom leans over with her legs stiff and her hands on her knees to look.

"It feels all right, Bud?"

"Sure. Scratchy, but I can scratch it now, see?"

He scratches to show her. "Going out back. You coming, Ray?" I don't feel like it right now.

"Have fun, Bud, and be careful," Mom says. So Bud limps like crazy going to the back door and she yells "Bud!" and he jumps up and down like a Yo-Yo, and runs out.

"He'll break it again for sure," she says. Which is probably true, but not for a few years, I hope. We don't need another of these confinements, that's for sure.

So I read a little and I fool around at the piano. No lessons during the summer. And I more or less just kill time, which is strange now that we're free. But I know why. Who am I kidding.

Finally he comes home. Dad comes home. Looks at me for a sec, then turns away. Big deal. He goes to the bathroom and locks the door and splashes water on his face and takes a leak, only he flushes the toilet at the same time so no one can hear. No kidding.

"Hi, Dad."

"Ray. Supper ready?"

"In a minute, Frank," Mom calls from the kitchen. "You two sit down. Bud. *Yooo,* Bud, time to come in for supper!"

My father slumps down in his dining-room chair, tilts back, sucks in his belly, and squeezes the edge of his napkin inside his trousers top. He at least takes it out of the napkin ring this time.

Okay. I look at him, right at him. Mom puts the

cold cuts on the table. Baloney, but she calls it cold cuts. I pour the milk. But I look at him, at his steamy spectacles, his thin black hair, his eyes that move around and light on things. I don't want to do this; I just feel like I have to, some way.

Bud zooms in, crouching down like Groucho Marx, and slides onto his chair. He wiggles his eyebrows at everybody.

Dad looks like he's choking. He isn't. We haven't even said grace, which we do at supper. He whips his napkin out, throws it on the table, looks at Bud's white leg swinging free and easy. Not at Bud, just the leg. He can't even talk. I'm ready this time, but it's hard to wait anyway. Jeez, it's hard, and I thought I was over that.

"Dad, Doc took it off this afternoon. He said it was time—"

"Not another word, Raymond. *Not another word!*"

"He said it was time for it to come off."

"I said not another *word,* and —"

"I *heard* you, I *heard* you. The whole damn *neighborhood* heard you, not that I give a damn!"

"Ray!"

"Well, they did, Mom."

Bud starts wailing like a police siren, which he's pretty good at. Dad just looks at the leg. He gets up and goes into the living room.

"Frank, come have your supper," Mom says.

He stomps around the living room. But not alone.

No sir, not this time. I stomp right with him. Like father, like son. Big stomper, little stomper. Besides, I'm not hungry. I feel like when they say "Runners, on your marks . . ."

And he stands, finally, and snaps his suspenders for a million years. He's so puffed up and mad that he's got tears in his eyes. Honest. Jeez, he might have a stroke right there by the—

"I don't know, Raymond, I just don't know what to make of it, but by God—"

"Don't know *what*. All we did was—"

"All *you* did, Raymond. All *you* did."

Oh jeez, I'm so damn sick of . . . Bud's on the davenport now, bouncing. Mom's standing by the dining-room arch.

"Well, Mom?"

"They asked me, Frank, and I gave my permission."

She takes off her apron and leans against the arch. She looks a little tired but not sleepy. She watches. Everybody watches everybody. It's spooky.

Dad stands there and then looks out the side window, not really looking *at* anything. I know that business. I'm supposed to crawl on my knees or something, and half the time I don't even know what's eating him, I swear. *This* time I do. Well, what the hell.

"Dad, look. Bud's fine and why can't we just—"

Blam! The floor. I'm on the floor! Grab the rocker arm. He twirled and hit me right in the head with the back of his hand, the bastard. Jeezus, wooo.

". . . thought you'd learned something."

I shake my head hard. Hurts. Hurt the hurt. Boy, I'm seeing stars.

Mom's in the room. "No, Bud. Frank, that's all and I *mean* it." She stands and holds Bud. He squirms and yells. Room goes around.

". . . could *depend* on him, but no, that's too much to . . ."

Damn broken record. There he is. Two of him, come together now. I'm on my knees. Shake my head again. Hands on his hips, mouth opening and shutting the same old record. Damn him, damn him, *damn* him.

Lunge. I lunge, run my head smack into his belly, and miss with my fists. Dizzy, wooo! He topples back into the overstuffed chair.

I see the ceiling upside down. Screaming? Not me. Him? Yah. Sucking in air. God, I'm tired. Tears, not for me. I got pain, okay, shaking, yah, but I'm all right.

He puffs. Red face. Arms waving like a turtle on its back.

*"So!"*

I look at the ceiling again, get it in focus. I sit up and breathe in as far as I can. Catch the last little ache and blow it out.

"So it's come to this."

Oh my God, he wet his pants. Just a little.

"But you hit me first and—"

112

"Accident, accident."

He won't do it again. I don't know how I know, but he won't do it again.

"Accident, my ass."

"Ray!" Mom says. "And, Frank, I'm not telling you again. Lord help us, that's *enough*. I'm calling Minneapolis."

I'm not happy but not scared either. Thought I'd be happy and maybe I am. I *should* be.

"Raymond, you listen and listen good. . . ."

"Listen *well*," Bud shouts. "*Well,* not good." He laughs and does his Groucho shuffle back to the davenport. "Right, Mom?"

"That's right."

"I didn't think that month was enough," Dad says.

"No, and I told the Reverend that."

"Thanks a lot, Dad."

He's shaking, he really is. Mom seems to be in the middle of the room. She's talking quietly, but you can hear every word. That's when you have to pay attention. Dad, too.

"So it's finally come, and who's at fault, Frank?" she says. "You've been asking for this, you know that. I . . . I hate to say this but you've had this coming, mister. Ray needs some breathing room right now and he's not going to get it here."

"Laura, I—"

"No, I'm certain of that. Frank, he's almost fourteen. I'm calling your mother, and Ray can—"

"Laura . . ."

She just looks at him and he stops. Sits there like a melted statue. Almost sad-looking. In a way, I feel sorry for him for just a minute.

Mom's so calm it's scary, like she was in a play or something. Like Joan Crawford or Bette Davis. Not the looks, just the way she acts. She gives Central the long-distance number. The call goes through fast and we all just wait without a sound except heavy breathing from Dad.

"Bertha," she says. She doesn't even sound like Mom. "Yes, I can hear fine. . . . Yes, Bud's doing well; the cast came off today. . . . I will, I'll tell him. Dear, how would it be with you folks if Ray came down? . . . Yes, for the rest of the summer. . . . That's right, right now."

Good Lord, things change in a hurry. Not bad, not bad at all. I'll miss out on some things here, but it's fun in Minneapolis, it really is. At their place.

"Yes, it is, Bertha. You're sure it won't be . . . I knew it, dear. . . . What? Yes, of course your son's here. Indeed he's here. . . . No, no, we're paying for this, you put that out of your mind. I'll write tomorrow. Here's Frank."

Dad doesn't move. Mom doesn't either, just holds the receiver and waits. So he saunters over and takes it. Bud watches all this with a grin like a jack-o'-lantern. Well, he deserves it, I guess. I don't know, I've kind of had enough for one day.

"Ma? Yes, this is Frank. How are you?"

The statue's alive and talking again.

"What? . . . Oh, fine, fine. Laura told you, I guess. We just thought it would be nice for Ray, and he's at that smart-aleck stage where . . ."

He walks, he talks, he crawls on his belly like a rep-tile.

"What? . . . Sure you can talk to him. Of course."

He goes back to the chair. Two jumps, headaches be damned, and I've got the receiver.

"Hi, Grandma! . . . Okay, how are you? . . . I'd like that. . . . No . . . really, I would, I'm not just being polite. . . . What? Tomorrow? Sure, and Bud says hi and it'll be good to see you both. Can I swim in Lake Nokomis? . . . Okay, sure, we'll talk it over. 'Bye."

Mom walks into the kitchen, Bud goes outside. I'm going to go up and pack some things. I hope Dad will . . . well, I don't know what. I try to catch his eye, but he's just standing by the window now with his forehead resting on the windowpane. Damn. If he'd only let up on a guy once in a while.

# 12

Well, the Greyhound to Minneapolis stops at Schweitzer's River Café at eight-thirty and Dad's going to meet me there. Or I'll meet *him;* he already went down to the store. Without a word.

Mom packed my suitcase last night and I rounded up my personal stuff, like a jackknife I usually carry, and a razor because it's getting so I have to shave every week now on my chin and Grandpa still uses a straightedge. Bud's walking down with me, so Mom checks my white shirt, straightens my tie, pats me on the cheek, and says, "Be good, Ray, and write us. We'll be down in August."

It's only a half mile or so from our house to the café but it seems ten times that long when you're wearing a white shirt and dragging a big leather suitcase on a summer morning. There isn't much time.

"Bud, you tell the guys where I'm going and have them write, okay? You know who to tell."

"Sure."

"And, Bud . . ."

"Yah."

"Keep your nose clean, okay?"

"What!"

"Forget it. Just an expression. It means be good."

"Oh, sure."

He's walking with one foot up on the curb and one in the gutter and he's quiet.

"Ray, can I come too?"

That's what it is. I knew he was thinking about something. I could tell last night.

"Not this time, Bud. I'll be back before you know it, and you'll come down when Mom and Dad come to pick me up."

"But I'll have to play with Maloney or get a dog or something."

"So? What's wrong with that? Playing with your own buddies, I mean. You know, go out to the slough and—"

"And the cave?"

"What cave? Oh, *that* cave. Yah. But you know, get to know them better, like I know Benson, see. I mean real pals."

"And Gladys?"

"No, not like I know Gladys."

We're here at the café. There's Dad. He hands me my ticket and we sit on revolving stools at the counter to wait. Bud whirls around and I watch Mabel, the waitress, draw coffee from the big coffee makers that look like shiny steel boilers. Dad looks down the row, and other men are lined up for their morning coffee. The big ceiling fan is turning already, but it doesn't even make a breeze; it just hums like it's cooler.

Dad has his coffee in front of him. The cup sits on a soggy paper napkin in the saucer. Mabel comes over.

"Ray, hi. So you're going to the big city! What's your brother's name?"

"Morgan," Bud says.

"No, it's Jefferson but everybody calls him Bud."

"Well, Bud," she says, "you going along and keep Ray company?"

"Nope. He won't let me."

Dad puts out his hand towards us without looking and pats the air, which is supposed to mean don't twirl, don't argue, don't talk, don't do anything.

"Ray, I got to go," Bud says.

"To the toilet?"

"No, home. I really *do*."

He means it. He doesn't look so much like a dog who's just been beaten.

"Well, sure, Bud. So long and take it easy now."

"So long, Ray. Maloney said he'd help me find the cave this summer and I almost forgot!" He runs out of the café and doesn't look back. Bud and Maloney. If there's a cave anywhere around there, those two will find it.

"He's cute," Mabel says.

"Yah, I guess. Don't say that to him though; he

kicks people in the shins."

"Well, I'll wait till he's a little older and out of the habit."

"Master Decker and Mr. Decker, I do declare."

It's Irv in for his coffee eye-opener. Says it gets him back in the land of the living and he'll never forgive it.

Dad turns. "Irv, I don't think—"

"Mr. Decker, I appreciate your opinions and your concern. I consider them abjectly wrong, but that's beside the point, and since I doubt that you want to hear more I'll just tarry long enough to wish my friend here a fond farewell until we meet again."

"So long, Irv. I'll see you."

"Always at your service." He shakes my hand hard. Feels good. Then he walks back through the café to the alley, yelling something about digestion to Mr. Schweitzer.

"Ray," Mabel says, "how about a glass of milk and a doughnut? Get your dad to spring for it."

"No thanks, I just had breakfast."

She stands and stretches like her back hurts, which it probably does. Then she shrugs and sweeps her arm, pointing all the way down the crowded counter and back into the booths.

"So did all these business barons, right, gentlemen? But that doesn't stop them from stoking up again. Oh well, you have a good time now."

"I will."

She can get away with it, poking fun at everybody, including Judge Trask. I heard her one day. She called him Judge Trash and got away with it.

Dad's awfully quiet. I know most of the fellows in here. They say things like "Hey, all dressed up for a trip to the Cities!" And "Don't do anything I wouldn't do . . . don't take any wooden nickels."

And then, doggone it all, Dad slaps me on the shoulder with his cigarette still in his hand and spills ashes down my shirt. But what gets me is he says, "Ray's got a vacation coming after all he did to help out with Bud, the little one. Broken leg, you know. Yessir, it'll be good for him."

And they all say, "Yah, sure," or "You bet," or "Have a swell time, Ray."

*Jeez,* why does he still have to put on the old act for the guys and . . . Well, he does, that's for sure. Why should I expect anything different?

There's the bus. I grab my bag and wait while a man and two women get off, probably to use the toilet. Dad stands out on the sidewalk and squints at the sun. He looks at me and says, "Going to be a hot one, Raymond. Hot as a pistol."

"Yah."

"So."

"Yah?"

"So be good."

He spins and walks next door to the store. I get a seat up front where I can watch the driver with those things on his legs like Royal Mounties. Bud would like those. The driver slams the door shut, takes my ticket, checks to see that everybody's back on the bus, and we roar and jerk to a start.

I can see Dad letting down the awning. He already looks hot. He turns while he's cranking and squints at the bus. I think he waved, probably. I'm almost sure he waved a little. I wave back like mad. Just before we turn the corner to grind up Semple Hill, he turns his back on the bus. Don't ask **me** why.